CAROLINE STORER

Being a poor sleeper, I've been making up stories for years now to try and exhaust my mind, and get some much needed sleep. It doesn't always work as the stories then demand to be written! I write mainly Historical romances, but I've also written Contemporary romances, Romantic Intrigue and I've also tried my hand at Futuristic and Time Slip romances.

I live on the beautiful island of Anglesey in North Wales, with my wonderful husband, Colin. By day I'm an Environmental Health Officer, where I get to meet lots of interesting people – all grist to the writer's mill.

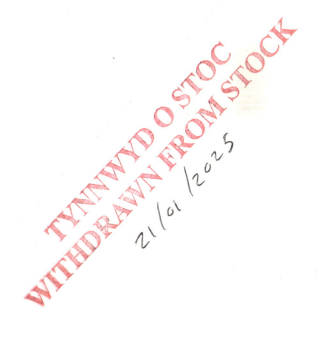

The Roman

CAROLINE STORER

Harper*Impulse* an imprint of
HarperCollinsPublishers Ltd
1 London Bridge Street
London SE1 9GF

www.harpercollins.co.uk

A Paperback Original 2015

First published in Great Britain in ebook format by Harper*Impulse* 2014

Cover images © Shutterstock.com

Caroline Storer asserts the moral right
to be identified as the author of this work

A catalogue record for this book is
available from the British Library

ISBN: 978-0-00-759160-2

This novel is entirely a work of fiction.
The names, characters and incidents portrayed in it are
the work of the author's imagination. Any resemblance to
actual persons, living or dead, events or localities is
entirely coincidental.

Automatically produced by Atomik ePublisher from Easypress

Firstly, I'd like to thank my editor, Charlotte Ledger, for giving me this wonderful opportunity to publish my book with HarperImpulse.

Secondly, I want to say a huge "thank you" to all my friends and family who have supported me, in particular my mum and dad, and best friends Kath and Paula.   I also want to mention all my cyber friends who, over the years, have given much needed help and encouragement.   Thank you, Suzanne, Michelle (Styles) and Kate (Hardy).

And finally...for my wonderful husband, Colin...who always believed.

CHAPTER ONE

Circus Maximus – Rome AD 79

Marsallas closed his eyes, letting the stillness inside the stables act as a balm to his ravaged senses. He could still hear the crowd in the arena chanting his name, even though he'd ridden his last race of the day.

For a full five minutes he stood there before he opened his eyes once more, and watched as his four horses, magnificent greys, were rubbed down by four slaves. Like him, the horses were quiet and still, allowing the slaves to tend them without any trouble. He walked over to them and stroked the muzzle of each of them in turn, his touch gentle and soothing. Lampon, the most forward of his horses, nudged him.

"Hah. You know me too well, Lampon," he said softly, taking a pear from a small cloth sack that he carried. The horse whinnied as he took the fruit, and Marsallas patted his flank before moving on to the other horses. When they had all been given their pears, Marsallas stood back, letting the slaves finish their tasks.

They were magnificent animals – he had chosen well – and they had not let him down once in the four years he'd had them. They had raced over two hundred races together, winning over one hundred and fifty of them in that time. A phenomenal feat, considering it was one of the most dangerous sports in the Circus Maximus. His *quadrigae* were considered the best, and when he raced his four-horse chariot he was always the favourite to win.

Once the slaves had finished tending to the horses, Marsallas dismissed them with a nod of his head, leaving him alone with his animals. He walked into each of the stalls and stroked his hands over the horses' flesh, feeling their muscles and ligaments to make sure there were no sprains or bruises. The sheer brutality of the races took its toll, on both man and beast, and it was Marsallas's duty to make sure that his horses were always kept in the best condition. Eventually he finished his rounds, and was closing the last of the doors to the stalls when he saw his team member and close friend, Fabius Rufus, coming towards him.

"Fabius," he said in greeting, a small smile on his face as his protégé approached. He was secretly proud of the young man; the man he had trained to be as good as him in the Circus. But then he frowned when he saw the preoccupied look on his face. "All is well, Fabius?"

"There is a woman here," Fabius said, by way of explanation, ignoring Marsallas's question. "She wants to see you. She has a slave with her—"

"Fabius," Marsallas interrupted, "I am not interested in entertaining the rich *patricians* of Rome tonight. I am tired, hungry and I stink. I'm going to bathe, eat and sleep in that order. Besides, even I have standards, and an orgy is just a little too debauched for my tastes!"

Fabius shook his head. "You're wrong, Marsallas. The slave is male and as large as a tree, and the woman just wants to talk to you, not seduce you."

"They always '*just want to talk*', Fabius," Marsallas grunted, shaking his head in vexation, "You should know *that* by now! We are nothing but studs to these women," then he turned towards the rear door of the stables. "By the gods, I'm sure the women of Rome are getting more and more forward these days."

2

"I agree with you, Marsallas, they are," Fabius reasoned, raising his voice slightly as Marsallas walked away. "But this time I think the woman is genuine. She says she has news—"

"Enough, Fabius," Marsallas shouted, cutting off his friend's words without a backward glance. "Like I said, you have her. All the women love your blonde hair and green eyes. *You* will have her eating out of your hand in next to no time!"

* * *

"You were quick. Didn't she live up to your expectations?" Marsallas asked a short while later, as he finished off a small meal of meat, bread and olives in his quarters.

Fabius's face suffused with colour as he stepped into the room and closed the door behind him. "No! I mean…I never…" Fabius stammered, his voice trailing off.

Marsallas raised an eyebrow in surprise. It was unusual for Fabius to be so nervous. Normally he was supremely confident when it came to women…and sex. "What ails you, Fabius? You seem out of sorts this evening."

"The woman. She just wants to see you. To talk to you."

"Fabius, how many times—"

"Justina." Fabius interjected, cutting off Marsallas. "She says her name is Justina, and she has come from Herculaneum."

The knife Marsallas had been using to slice some meat was stabbed into the wooden table with such force that the handle wobbled violently. His eyes narrowed in anger, as his brain assimilated the full implication of Fabius's words. An ominous silence fell between the two men until, finally, Marsallas stood, the scraping of his chair sounding as loud as a thunderbolt.

"Where is she?" he hissed, the words forced past tight lips, his face pinched with anger.

"Outside."

Marsallas said nothing for a moment as his mind raced

3

frantically. He stared at the wooden door, as if he could actually see through it. Justina was here. Outside and waiting for him. He felt his stomach clench, and he forced down the wave of nausea that threatened at the thought of meeting her again. Conflicting emotions surged though him. Anger vied with despair. Rage battled hope. But it was *fear* that took precedence. Because fear was a double-edged sword…

Fear could make him lose what little control he had over his emotions when it came to Justina; emotions he had ruthlessly tried to suppress for years now. Fear could make him lash out, to try and hurt *her* as much as she had hurt *him*, or equally, it could make him do something totally out of character, like pull her into his arms and kiss her. Because when it came to Justina, she made him *think* and *feel* things he'd never felt for *any* woman.

For six years long years he'd desperately tried to wipe her from his memory. Sometimes he succeeded, often going weeks without thinking about her. But then something would happen, a jolt to his memory, and he would find himself once more wondering about her…remembering her…

Justina. The only woman he'd ever loved…and the only woman he'd ever hated. She'd taken his love and thrown it back in his face, and in the space of one day she had systematically destroyed him. Her betrayal had turned the young, untried man he'd once been, and made him into the cold, hard, bastard he was today.

And now she was here, waiting outside his quarters, wanting an audience with him. He couldn't help but wonder if the six years since he'd last seen her had wrought many changes in her. She would be twenty-two now, a far cry from the sixteen-year-old girl he'd known back then.

But that girl had been so beautiful, and he closed his eyes briefly as he remembered what she had looked like. He could picture her as clearly now as if it had only been yesterday since he'd last seen her, instead of all those years ago. Tall and slim, she'd had the palest of skin, which had been so soft to the touch. Skin that had been in stark contrast to her jet-black hair, and he remembered teasing her about her heritage, saying she must be descended from a warrior woman enslaved from the wild north lands. Her features had been perfection too, from her wide grey eyes down over her small, straight nose to the fullest lips he'd ever seen. Lips that he'd had the urge to kiss, from the first moment he'd seen them...

Marsallas re-opened his eyes, focusing on the present once more as he weighed up the situation he was now faced with. The *rational* side of him said that he should just send her away, refuse her request. But the *irrational* side of him wanted to see her again. It would be a test of sorts, he decided. If she elicited no response in him other than disdain then he would know for *certain* that he had finally managed to purge her from his mind once and for all.

The *irrational* won…

So he sat down, pulled out the knife that was embedded in the wood, and carried on slicing another piece of meat. Deliberately, he kept his posture relaxed, giving nothing away of the inner turmoil he was experiencing, before finally saying to Fabius, "Tell her to come in. I will see her."

* * *

"If I am not out in five minutes knock on the door. It will be my signal to leave."

Diogenes frowned, but said nothing, just stared down at her.

Justina smiled slightly, interpreting his look, well used to the slave's silence. "I will be fine. I promise."

Diogenes stood aside and Justina tapped on the door. Without waiting for an answer she pushed it open and entered the dark room.

At first she thought there was no one there, Fabius having played her false by sending her into an empty room. With only one wall sconce illuminating the room, most of the space was in darkness. But then she saw a slight movement, and as she let her eyes adjust to the dimness, she was able to make out the shadow of a man standing as still as marble to the rear of the room.

Then the shadow spoke. "Justina."

The emotionless tone of the voice caused Justina to shiver, and her heart to beat faster. There was no mistaking who had said her name. His voice was indelibly printed on her mind. But the tone was deeper than it had once been, rough almost. Yet it had a pleasing quality she couldn't explain.

Uninvited, she walked further into the room, his presence drawing her to him like an invisible bond, only stopping when she approached the edge of a small table. She glanced down at the remains of a meal, then back up to where the shadow stood. Lifting her head towards him, she said as calmly as she could, "Greetings, Marsallas."

Then the shadow stepped forward, suddenly becoming human flesh, and Justina gasped, her face losing all colour as she took in the man standing in front of her.

There was no doubting it was Marsallas. But at the same time she couldn't believe how much he'd changed. He was virtually unrecognisable from the carefree youth she had once known. Now, in his place stood a virtual stranger, one who looked at her with a look of total indifference on his face.

He looked even taller than she remembered, if that were possible. Broad shoulders tapered down to bare arms, tanned a golden brown; arms that were crossed over each other, showing off his powerfully bunched muscles. Of their own free will her eyes tracked down his body. Over the impressive width of his chest, which couldn't be disguised by the short green tunic he wore, down past the tautness of his flat stomach, to his long, tanned muscular legs.

Justina felt a quiver of awareness slither down her spine, and like a starving woman she feasted on him; the hard sculpted face, the piercing blue eyes she remembered so well. She drank him in, absorbed him, and her fingers actually itched to caress the hard planes of his face, to trace the shape of his eyebrows and the angled hardness of his jaw.

She felt his power. Not just his physical power, but the sheer presence of him. Although he had only said one word, his bearing said it all, and it made her stomach clench. Even now, after all these years, he still had the power to affect her, and without warning a sudden surge of longing, long suppressed, assailed her.

She saw his eyes lower to her mouth. She hadn't been kissed in years, and she felt desire flare deep inside of her, rising to such an intensity it fairly took her breath away. She ached for him to draw her nearer, to kiss her, to stroke her body to life once more.

Then she saw his eyes narrow, harden, and Justina felt a rush of panic hit her. She was stupid to have come here.

She should have gone back to Herculaneum and lied to Quintus, said she'd tried to gain an audience with Marsallas, but he had refused to see her. But she hadn't, and instead she was standing no more than ten feet from him.

Totally at his mercy.

She wanted to flee, but she held her ground. Instead, she straightened her spine and prepared herself for the ordeal that was to come.

And it would be an ordeal.

She forced a polite smile, desperate to keep to the plan she had mentally prepared whilst standing outside his quarter's, waiting for Fabius to introduce her. *Just go in.* She had said, over and over again, like a mantra. *Be cordial, say what you have to say, and then get out of there as quickly as you can.*

"Thank…thank you for letting me see you. What…what I have to say won't take long. I—"

"You have come a long way to see me, Justina, considering I said I never wanted to see you again," Marsallas drawled, his mouth twisting in derision as he interrupted her faltering words. "*And* if my memory serves me right, I cursed you to Hades too."

Justina felt a sudden chilling panic pierce her, but she kept her face impassive, refused to let him see how much he disturbed her. So she kept her hands loosely clasped in front of her, and made herself relax. She lifted her chin, hoping he wouldn't notice the faint trembling of her body that she couldn't quite control, "I do remember, Marsallas," she said, keeping her voice steady, "But I am not here to see you, I have come because I have a message from your uncle. Quintus is—"

She heard his breath hiss, before he cut off her well-rehearsed speech with a violent slash of his hand. "Stop!"

She froze. Helpless. Unable to think, or do anything, she watched as he lowered his hand, her eyes taking in his long narrow fingers, fingers that Justina remembered so well…

"I do not want to hear about him – ever."

His words were harsh, but Justina felt a surge of pity for him. She knew how much he hated his uncle, and secretly she couldn't blame him. His uncle had never shown his nephew any love.

The words hung heavily between them, and wisely she said nothing, as she could see that he was holding onto his anger by a thin thread. His face was an implacable mask, devoid of emotion, and for several long moments he stared at her, his eyes unfathomable as he watched her. Then he stepped forward, and this time she couldn't control her bodily reaction.

She shivered inwardly, when the warmth of his fingers cupped her chin, exerting enough pressure that she had no choice but to lift her face up to his. For years she dreamt of feeling his touch again, and now he was so close that she could feel the heat of his breath on her face, see the flecks of blue colour that made up his magnificent eyes. She had to fight the urge to close her eyes when the warm scent of his skin, a mixture of sandalwood and musk, floated over her, enveloping her like a cloak, bringing back memories long suppressed. Heat pooled in the pit of her stomach, as delicious sensations curled through her.

Then his fingers splayed out, and she had to bite back a groan of desire. Two of his fingers still cupped her chin, but the others feathered softly down the slim column of her throat, before they came to rest on the pulse that beat rapidly at the base of her throat.

This time the heat within her spread to every pore of her skin, making her hot and dewy, feverish almost, and when she saw the pupils of his eyes dilate, she could tell he was very much aware of her reaction to him.

The moment was broken when he casually dropped his hand and stood back from her, breaking off all bodily contact. Inwardly she mourned the loss of his touch. A touch that brought back so many memories.

"You must be fatigued after your long journey. Would you like some refreshment?"

The sudden change of tone in his voice unnerved her. Gone was the anger, now there was a mocking edge to it, and Justina had to press her lips together to prevent her from saying anything. Deliberately she lowered her eyes, in case they showed any hint of defiance. She didn't want to antagonise him, couldn't afford to bait him in any way, she knew that.

That would be foolish. And she wasn't a fool.

Desperate to recover her composure, she looked up at him with what she hoped was a neutral expression on her face. "No thank you. I had something to drink at the inn before I came here."

"Do you mind if I do?"

Justina bit down on her lip in irritation. "*Yes*," she wanted to shout, "*I do mind.*" But she held back her words. She knew he was playing some sort of twisted game. Teasing her, like a cat teased a mouse.

Shaking her head slightly, she smiled politely, "No, of course not."

But when he moved closer to her, to lean across the table to pour some wine into a goblet, she lost all ability to think. Once again the heady scent of his skin brought back memories, and she closed her eyes briefly, remembering everything about him as if the past six years had only been yesterday.

It was only when she opened her eyes and saw him watching her, with eyes so fathomless, that she realised he knew *exactly* what he was doing to her.

Justina blushed in mortification. How could he have affected her so quickly? She should be immune to him after all these years. She told herself to turn and leave, get out of there as fast as possible, but her body was incapable of moving.

Eventually Marsallas broke the tension by raising his goblet in an unspoken mocking salute, before he drowned the contents in one swallow, never once taking his gaze off her.

Justina watched him, biting the inside of her lip. If she needed proof that coming here was a mistake, then his false gesture was the final bit of evidence she needed. He wasn't interested in anything she had to say. She could see that in every hard line of his body, by the coldness radiating out of his eyes.

Whatever emotions he had once felt for her had long gone; wiped out by six years of bitterness.

She had to leave. Right now. And without a second thought about the actual reason *why* she was here, she turned and bolted for the door, and hopefully, her escape.

She thought she had succeeded. Her hand was on the rounded wooden door knob, and the door had even opened slightly. But then she saw two hands slam above her head' banging the door shut, trapping her between his two outstretched arms.

How had he moved so fast? She thought, panic coursing through her as she tried ineffectually to wrench open the door.

"Don't go." The words were whispered in her ear, so intense, so passionate that she felt her heart break right open.

Swallowing past the lump of emotion in her throat, she whispered, "I have to go, Marsallas. I shouldn't have come. It was a mistake. I…I'm sorry."

Still desperate to escape, and in what she knew to be a futile effort, she tried to pull open the door. But the door didn't move, and with mounting desperation she lifted her hands, her nails digging into the hard muscles and tendons of Marsallas's forearms trying to pull them away.

But the door stayed shut, her strength no match for his, as he leaned his weight against the wood barring her escape. Eventually she stopped, her hands dropping to her sides, her chest rising and falling with exertion as if she had run for miles.

For several long moments she stood there, her mind racing, desperately wondering what to do next. She needed to be strong, not let him see how much his presence had affected her, how much she still desired him. To show him would be foolish – suicidal – even. Then, a different feeling came over her and she realised that she was actually frightened of him.

She didn't know *why* he frightened her. Maybe it was because he had changed so much in the intervening years since she had last seen him. Not just physically, but mentally too. The youth she had known had only ever shown her kindness. But now, today, she wasn't so sure. He looked so hard, indomitable, the coldness of his blue eyes revealing so much more about him than what he'd actually said.

The man that stood behind her was the product of his uncle's hatred – and hers – if she were honest. She, and Quintus, had made him the man he was today. But she knew, deep down, that Marsallas wouldn't hurt her. He might *hate* her, but he wouldn't *harm* her. Marsallas wasn't like his uncle, she was sure of that.

Then thinking of Quintus, and all she had suffered at his hands these past years, she mentally squared her shoulders and turned slightly, as if to convey to Marsallas that she wasn't afraid of him.

But her rational thoughts disappeared instantly, when by turning, she brought herself even closer to him, if that were possible. Her heart skipped a beat when she felt Marsallas's breath on her neck, moist and hot as he leaned in even closer, a soft sigh escaping him.

"Yes," he whispered, as his mouth made contact with the warm skin of her neck. With deliberately slow movements he took hold of her hand, and turned her fully, so she now faced him. He was so close, the heady scent of his skin so intoxicating, that she couldn't stop the shiver of arousal that coursed through her.

No more than two minutes had passed since she had entered his quarters, and already her body was reacting to him like it had always done. It was as if her emotions, which she had ruthlessly suppressed all these years, had suddenly erupted like some dormant volcano, and her desire for him – her longing for him – burst forth like molten lava, threatening to overwhelm her.

She heard him laugh softly under his breath, as if he knew *exactly* what she was feeling, what she was experiencing. And when he moved closer, so his hips made contact with hers, Justina groaned inwardly as she felt the hardness of his arousal nudging her lower belly.

"Beautiful, beautiful, Justina. I want you."

Justina's eyes widened. *Had she heard him correctly?* Shaking her head in denial she whispered, "No… I…" But her words trailed off when he bent his head, and felt his tongue stroke the sensitive area of her neck just under her earlobe. Heat curled in the pit of her stomach; warmth spreading through her whole body, as her knees went weak with longing.

"You say 'no', but your body screams 'yes' Justina. You can deny it all you want, but you want me as much as I want you. I felt it earlier when I caressed your neck. Your beating pulse told me everything I needed to know." The words were soft, a rumbling from deep within his chest as his teeth nipped the soft lobe of her ear, the sensations so intense that she couldn't stop herself from arching her neck.

Eventually, reality returned, and instinctively she tried to pull away. "Marsallas no! Stop, please. Please—"

But he ignored her plea, and his mouth closed over hers, his lips bruising as he kissed her with deliberate passion. Justina tried to turn her head away, to escape the onslaught of his mouth. But his fingers burrowed under her long hair, trapping her, forcing her to stay where she was, as his hand curved around the back of her neck pulling her towards him.

The kiss intensified, as if he were stamping his presence on her, punishing her for all the years of torment she had put him through.

She moaned, hating the rough assault of his mouth on hers, her nails digging into the hard muscles of his forearms as she tried to pull away.

But her resistance was futile, her strength no match against his, as Marsallas pressed his hips into the softness of her stomach, the gesture blatantly sexual. Again Justina moaned, remembering how it had once been between them. How he had kissed her so softly, so gently, that she had wanted the kiss to go on forever.

Then as quickly as it began, the kiss ended.

Marsallas pulled away from her, and Justina turned her head in mortification, not daring to look at him. She heard his ragged breathing as he stood there, the sound harsh in the stillness of the room. Once again she felt her chin being lifted, her eyes forced to meet his. Expecting to see hatred reflected there, she was taken aback when, instead, she saw torment and pain in the darkness of his eyes.

Justina felt her resistance crumble. *Had he hated kissing her like that? Did he remember what it had once been like between them?*

The questions flew through her mind. She wanted to ask him, but she was incapable of speech. Instead, she lifted her hand and laid it along his strong jaw bone, conveying to him without words, what she was thinking, what she was feeling.

The unspoken gesture was enough and she closed her eyes as Marsallas's mouth fused with hers once more.

"Justina," he breathed, and this time he kissed her in a way that sent heat searing through her body. This time his lips weren't trying to punish – they were gentle, soft, mobile – seducing her, awakening memories of long ago when they shared such sweet kisses together.

His hands reached for her once more, gently caressing, skimming

13

over the slimness of her shoulders, downwards, until they rested on the sides of her ribcage. Slowly, they moved inwards, cupping the fullness of her breasts, and Justina jerked, feeling the sensitive flesh swell, her nipples pebbling with desire as he rubbed them through the thinness of her silk gown. Long-suppressed sensations flushed into life, as she gloried in the feel of his hands on her body once more.

"Marsallas," she groaned against his lips, wanting so much more.

"You want me, don't you?" he whispered.

"Yes. Oh yes—"

Then reality hit her, as the full implication of what she was saying, what she was doing, impinged on her passion-soaked mind. This time it was *she* who pulled away, and as she stared at him, time seemed suspended as Marsallas watched her, his face giving nothing away.

She felt shaken to the core by what had just happened, both of them caught up in the past and the present. Then, mercifully, the tension was broken by a loud rap on the door, the noise as loud as a thunder-clap in the stillness of the room.

Diogenes! Of course! She realised belatedly. Her allotted time with Marsallas was up. The interruption broke the tension between them, and she whispered, "I…I have to go. Quintus—"

She realised her mistake as soon as she uttered Quintus's name when his face darkened and his eyes narrowed into dark slits of anger. Then he turned abruptly and walked away from her, returning to the table to pour another goblet of wine.

"Yes. Go now while you can, Justina. I'm sure my uncle has need of you." The words were hissed past tight lips, before he turned to her once again, his face closed, unreadable.

Justina said nothing. She wanted to run over to him, beg his forgiveness and explain everything.

But she didn't.

Instead she turned and wrenched open the door, leaving the room with as much dignity as she could, holding back the tears that threatened to fall.

It was only when she heard a loud smash come from Marsallas's quarters that her step faltered. Marsallas must have thrown his wine goblet on the floor in anger or frustration – or both...

* * *

Marsallas tapped the table with his index finger, looking up with bloodshot eyes to where Fabius sat opposite him.

Fabius raised his eyebrows, but said nothing. Doing as Marsallas asked, he refilled his goblet with wine once more.

"You have three races tomorrow, Marsallas. Is it wise to get so drunk?"

Marsallas pulled a wry smile and looked up at his friend, "Are you my mother now, Fabius?" he asked, his words slurred, and not waiting for an answer he lifted the goblet and drowned the contents in one giant gulp.

"No, not your mother," laughed Fabius, "But maybe your conscience. You, my friend, are going to have a mighty sore head in the morning." And this time, without being asked, Fabius filled the goblet once more.

But instead of drinking the wine, Marsallas merely stared down at the rich liquid, his mouth twisting, his mind racing. A long silence fell between the two men, both of them lost in their own thoughts until Marsallas broke it by muttering, "She is as slim and beautiful as I remember. It would have been something if she had gone to *fat!*"

Marsallas looked up at Fabius, seeing the slight smile on the younger man's face. He grunted slightly, his own mouth twisting into a smile of sorts. "I've said that before haven't I?"

"Aye. A few times this evening."

Then as quickly as it came, Marsallas's smile vanished. "I wanted to hate her, Fabius. But instead I kissed her," he said, his voice thick with emotion. He saw Fabius's eyebrows shoot up in surprise at his words. "See, I have shocked you now, eh?"

Fabius nodded, before he leaned forward, "She told me she is staying at the inn near the Forum. She leaves tomorrow, after the fifth hour."

Marsallas assimilated that bit of news without responding, and another silence fell between them, both of them oblivious to the raucous laughter behind them as they sat at their table in the drinking den.

"Was she your lover, Marsallas? In...in Herculaneum? Is that why she came here to see you?" Fabius finally asked, several minutes later.

For several long seconds Marsallas said nothing. He desperately wanted to say "yes" to Fabius. To tell him that Justina had once been his lover in the true sense of the word. But that would be a lie. All he'd had ever done was kiss her, caress her, nothing more.

He lifted his head, eventually meeting Fabius's curious gaze. "You couldn't be further from the truth if you tried, my friend. Justina was never my lover. She's my uncle's *mistress*!"

CHAPTER TWO

Justina looked out of the window, and stared down into the crowded Forum for what must have been the hundredth time. *Patricians*, *plebeians*, merchants and slaves all going about their daily business, totally oblivious of the woman who watched them all with anxious eyes.

Would he come? The time was approaching for her and Diogenes to leave, but she wanted to wait until the last possible moment before she returned to Herculaneum, just in case he turned up.

She worried her bottom lip with small white teeth, thinking about their meeting yesterday. He had looked at her with such hatred, but then he had kissed her with such passion, and then such tenderness, that she had been overwhelmed. And when the kiss had ended, and she'd left his quarters, frustration had eaten away at her for failing to explain anything to him. But then what had she expected? It was obvious that he still loathed the very sight of her after all these years.

Justina sighed, and moved away from the window back to the bed. She finished packing the small amount of clothes she had brought with her, the chore taking her mind off the long journey ahead of her, and the conversation she would be required to have with Quintus. She dreaded what his reaction would be, once she

17

told him that she had failed to persuade Marsallas to return. And even though she knew he would be too weak to retaliate, Quintus *still* managed to cause her stomach to clench in fear. And, of course, he still had Secundus to do his bidding…

Just thinking of Quintus's cruel, and hated, overseer caused her to shiver in repulsion. Secundus acted as Quintus's right-hand man, effectively running the villa, and had done so ever since Quintus's gradual decline in health several years ago meant he couldn't control his slaves – and her – as he used to. But Secundus was even crueller than Quintus, if that were possible, and he meted out such horrific punishments on any of the slaves that incurred his wrath, that even Quintus had, on occasions, had to intervene and tell him to stop, such were the extent of their injuries.

He'd also been her nemesis these past two years, ever since he had arrived at the villa. He watched her every movement, his snake-like eyes missing nothing as they stripped her body bare, and he always seemed to be near her, waiting for any excuse to touch her. It had become so unbearable at times that she had even been forced to inform Quintus. Thankfully, Quintus had warned him off, and the touching had stopped for a while, but then slowly, insidiously, it would start all over again. And Justina knew he was only biding his time, waiting for Quintus to die, before he made his final move and took what he wanted. Her. In his bed. Justina's lips twisted wryly as she thought of the potential danger she was in. How ironic, she thought, that for six years she'd managed to avoid Quintus's touch, only to find herself at the mercy of his overseer.

Justina shuddered and deliberately dismissed him from her thoughts. She needed to finish packing if she were to be ready to leave at the allotted time, and worrying about Secundus wasn't going to solve anything. She would just have to deal with him when the time came. And she would. Because once Quintus was dead, she would be a free woman, a woman who would finally be in control of her life…and her destiny.

A few minutes later she was ready, and when she heard a knock at the door she walked over to it and opened it, assuming it would be Diogenes come to collect her. But her body froze when she saw Marsallas leaning against the door frame watching her, a brooding look on the harsh planes of his face.

For a moment she remembered the young man of her youth and mourned his demise, for the man standing across the room from her bore no resemblance to the youth she had known all those years ago. And although he had been muscular as a young man, today, as he stood there in the doorway of her room looking totally at ease, Justina had to admit that he had matured into an outstanding specimen of manhood.

The life as a charioteer demanded peak physical fitness, and Justina had to acknowledge that he looked every inch the superb athlete that he must be. *And* he looked totally at ease in his skin, as if he knew *exactly* what effect he had on women.

Unbidden, he came slowly into the room, smiling a wolf's smile, and Justina blushed at having been caught staring at him again. He lifted his arms in a gesture of supplication, the action faintly mocking, as his blue gaze fixed on hers with such intensity that it caused Justina's stomach to clench partly in fear and partly in response to the sheer masculinity he exuded.

"So here I am. What was so important that you had to travel to Rome to see me?"

Justina swallowed, her nerves on edge, as he came further into the room, his muscular presence instantly shrinking it. She felt her breath catch as he came closer, standing no more than three feet away from her. The harsh lines of his face had been carved out by his life in the Circus. But he was also ruggedly handsome, and just looking at him caused her heart to beat erratically even after all the years away from him.

She had the urge to move away, to put some distance between them, but didn't want to appear a coward, so instead she lifted her chin and looked him squarely in the eyes. Her fear dissipated somewhat when she saw, with some surprise, that he looked ill.

His skin was a sallow yellow colour, his eyes bloodshot and she could see sweat beading on his forehead and upper lip. Concern overcame fear and she ignored his question. Instead she asked, "Are you ill?"

She saw him raise an eyebrow, and a small smile appeared at the corner of his mouth.

"Your concern is touching, Justina. No, I am not ill, just recovering from the excesses of last night, if you know what I mean. Life as one of Rome's great charioteers is just one long endless party."

Justina blushed at the sarcastic tone of his voice and she turned away, annoyed with herself for showing concern for him. She should have realised that he would turn it against her.

After a tense silence had fallen in the room, she turned back to him and saw him watching her through narrowed eyes. He was obviously still waiting for an answer as to why she had come to see him, so taking a deep breath she said in a measured tone, "Your uncle is dying. I've come to Rome to ask you to return to Herculaneum. To…to come home."

Another long silence descended in the room until Marsallas barked, "Home! Since when has that mausoleum ever been a home? No, I don't think so, Justina. You can tell my uncle that I am far too busy here in Rome!"

Justina said nothing. She didn't argue with him or try to persuade him as she knew it would be futile. She had, at least, carried out the order she had been given, and could now return to Herculaneum knowing that she had spoken with him. If she was honest with herself, she agreed with Marsallas. In all the years she had lived in the vast villa, she had never felt comfortable, and she had prayed every day for the opportunity to be presented to her so she could leave the cold, austere place.

"Tell me one thing though, Justina." Marsallas asked, breaking into her thoughts, "Did my uncle *ask*, or *order* you to come here?"

Justina looked up at him, guilt stealing over her, as hot colour stained her cheeks at his question. The unspoken reaction was answer enough for Marsallas, and he laughed, the sound harsh and guttural in the silence of the room. "Just as I thought," he said, his mouth twisting in derision. "No, I will not come back to Herculaneum, Justina. My life there is over, you can tell my uncle that. It was over the day he *bedded* you!"

She stiffened at the harshness of his words, but said nothing, watching as he walked back towards the door, and back out of her life once more. But then he stopped abruptly, as if he had suddenly remembered something, before he turned and walked back to where she stood. She had to resist the urge to flee when she saw the intense look on his face as he came towards her. However she stood her ground, willing her body to remain calm. But when he came to within touching distance of her she was potently aware of his raw sexuality. Her skin prickled in awareness, and she swallowed hard, her throat suddenly dry. She could well imagine the women of Rome wanting him in their beds.

"I almost forgot," he murmured softly, lifting up her chin with firm fingers, and Justina not having any choice, looked up into his face. She felt her eyelashes flutter slightly as her eyes clashed with his. His fingers were rough, calloused, with the hard work of his life. Then she felt his thumb skim over the fullness of her bottom lip, and she had to fight the urge to taste his skin with her tongue. She could see resistance in his eyes as he touched her, as if he were fighting his own internal battles as far as she was concerned. Then his eyes darkened with suppressed passion, and before she could think, or react, he leaned forward and took her in his arms and kissed her – deeply – his lips firm and unyielding, his tongue demanding and gaining access to the softness within.

Justina gripped his strong, bare forearms, wanting to break away from the kiss, but unable to do so as a surge of desire flowed through her. She closed her eyes, caught up in the headiness of his mouth on hers. Eventually he pulled away and Justina felt bereft that the kiss had ended so soon. But then the enormity of what had just happened hit her, and her eyes flew open.

21

For a heartbeat neither of them moved, but then Marsallas broke the spell between them, his lip twisting in derision. He cocked his head and clicked his tongue, in what was obviously a false gesture of regret, before asking in a mocking tone, "Tell me, do I kiss better than Quintus?"

Justina gasped in horror at his words, and before she could think, she slapped him across the face. Hard.

For a moment she couldn't believe she'd hit him, and she stood open-mouthed with shock at her audacity. She watched as a large red mark appeared on his cheek, before stepping backwards in an involuntary movement when she saw his eyes narrow in anger.

"Witch," Marsallas hissed, a nerve ticking furiously along his clenched jawline. For a moment Justina thought he might retaliate, but he didn't. Instead, he turned and strode out of the room without a backward glance, the door slamming shut behind him.

* * *

Diogenes came into the room a short while later. Justina was sitting on the bed deep in thought. She looked up at the silent man; reading the question in his eyes, the concern on his face.

"I will be ready in a moment, Diogenes," she murmured, standing up. Then, in a sudden surge of rebellion, against Quintus and his orders, she said, "But we are not leaving for Herculaneum just yet. I want to go to the Circus Maximus first."

* * *

"*Mar-sall-as! Mar-sall-as!*" The name rang around the vast arena, bouncing off the sides in a cacophony of noise, so deafening that Justina had to put her fingers in her ears to block it out. There must have been nearly one hundred thousand people in the arena, and it seemed that all of them were chanting his name over and over again, shouting and screaming in mass hysteria, as their hero

22

rode his victory lap. Justina, caught up in it all, watched spellbound, as her eyes followed his every move as he rode around the arena acknowledging the approval of the crowd.

He had just won his race – yet again – and had been "crowned" with his palm branch and wreath, whilst the four horses he drove were adorned with palm branches attached to their harnesses. The horses seemed to know that they were being worshipped and pranced and preened as they trotted around the arena, absorbing the accolades meted out on both man and beast.

Justina could see that Marsallas was revered with some sort of cult status, and she would have had to be blind not to see the covert looks all the women gave him. It was obvious that he could have any of the women here with a snap of his fingers, but as he waved to the crowd, his stance strong and proud as he stood in his chariot guiding his horses, Justina could see that his face was grim, and she wondered why he wasn't revelling in his victory…

They had not long arrived, and had just taken their seats so she and Diogenes had missed most of the race, but now as she looked around at the crowds she could tell that they were obviously enjoying themselves. Eventually the crowd quietened as Marsallas finished his victory lap and rode out of the arena and everyone took their seats. The intense rays of the afternoon sun beat down mercilessly, and Justina wiped the sweat from her brow. *How on earth did people manage to stay here all day in this heat* she wondered?

She leant across and asked a young couple sitting next to them how the races were run, explaining that she was a visitor to Rome, and once they realised she was a novice to the games needed no further invitation, being more than happy to explain the "rules" to her. She was told that there were four teams – factions – the Blues, Greens, Whites and Reds, and obviously, from the colour of his tunic, Marsallas rode for the Blues. Apart from his tunic the only other adornments he wore were *fasciae* – padded bonds that were wrapped around his torso and thighs for protection, a thick leather helmet that protected his head and a *falx* – a curved knife – to cut the reins that were wrapped around his hands in case of an accident if he was dragged around the arena.

Apparently, she had missed the elaborate opening ceremony that consisted of a procession led by the dignitaries who were sponsoring the games, followed by the charioteers and teams, musicians, dancers and priests carrying the statues of the gods and goddesses who watched over the races. Once the procession had finished the charioteers drew lots for their position in the starting gates, and once the horses were ready, a white cloth – *mappa* – was dropped by the sponsor of the games. At the signal, the gates were sprung, and up to twelve teams of horses thundered onto the track and the spectators followed the race by watching the bronze dolphin counters being pulled down on the *spina* – located on the central barrier after each lap passed.

"Is Marsallas competing again?" She asked the young woman.

The woman nodded, "Yes. He rides at least three races a day on average, sometimes up to five."

"Five!" Justina exclaimed.

"Aye. He is fabulously rich, you know, he earns a fortune – some say he has amassed over twenty million *sesterces* in the last six years or so he has raced! He has never been injured, either, it is a miracle really."

At Justina's shocked expression, the woman giggled and leaned forward to whisper in her ear, "Rich, handsome *and* unmarried, it is a shame I am a married woman, if you know what I mean. He can have any woman he wants, rich or poor, slave or *patrician*. And frequently does, if the gossips are to be believed!"

Justina felt a surge of jealousy flow through her at the woman's words, but never had the chance to reply, even if she had wanted to, as the crowd surged to its feet once more, the trumpeters announcing that another race was about to start. As she craned her neck towards the starting gates she could see that Marsallas was once again racing, as he stood proud and erect in his chariot. He must be exhausted, she thought, a worried frown on her face, but

24

the race started, and the thunder of the horse's hooves, as well as the roar of the crowd, took over, cutting off her wayward thoughts.

As she watched entranced, she could see that Marsallas was a master tactician and knew exactly what he was doing as he rode at breakneck speed around the area. He used his body weight, his reins tied around his torso, to lean from side to side to direct his horses' movements, keeping his hand free for the whip he carried. She could see that there were other chariots sporting the blue colours, and it seemed as if they all worked as a team, the other charioteers using various tactics to break the concentration of their opponents, which then allowed their team mates to gain the coveted inside of the track, maximising their chances of winning.

Marsallas controlled his horses with what seemed to be the minimum amount of effort, almost with an arrogance that bordered on dangerous, as if he didn't care whether he won or not. Whether he lived or died—

The crowd gasped, as one of the opposing charioteers – a White – was forced against the inside wall of the arena. His chariot broke apart as it smashed into the stone wall and he was thrown from it. Justina could hardly bear to watch as the poor man was dragged around the ring still holding onto the horses' reigns, until, finally he was able to bring the horses to a stop. She let out a sigh of relief when she saw that he seemed to be unharmed as he stood up and ran out of the way of the oncoming chariots that had already raced around the track and were now on their way to the finishing line.

Her eyes focused back on Marsallas's chariot, and she could see that he was once again in the lead, having held his team of horses back until the last minute to keep them from exhaustion, before allowing them full reign and letting them race as fast as they wanted to. She marvelled at his skill, as he rode around the arena at breakneck speed, seemingly totally unconcerned by the danger he must face every time he raced, and Justina was amazed that he had never been injured. She watched, with a sense of relief, when he passed the finishing line, again the winner, before once again acknowledging the adoration of the crowd as he undertook his victory lap.

Once the race finished Justina let out a huge sigh, relieved that he had escaped injury, and sat back down heavily onto the wooden seat, feeling totally exhausted. She smiled wryly to herself, thinking that if Marsallas knew of her concern for him, he would have reacted with scorn, no doubt throwing it back in her face.

She recalled how different it had once been between them. There had been no bitterness, no hatred, no anger between them.

And then, as if the past had suddenly come right back to haunt her, she remembered how it had all started...

CHAPTER THREE

Herculaneum – AD 73
Six Years Earlier...

Justina sighed, stood up and wiped the sand off her hands on the coarse linen of her *stola*, a frown on her face as she stared down at the sand sculpture. She tilted her head slightly. It wasn't her best effort, she thought, pulling a face of disgust. She had been trying to sculpt a life-size figure of a deer in full flight. But she hadn't quite got the proportions right, she decided. The head was too big for the body and the legs were too long and skinny.

She had got the idea for the sculpture from a fresco she had seen on the wall of the Basilica a few days ago and had been itching to sculpt it ever since. She had memorised the drawing, but obviously not well enough. But then, she realised, perhaps she was being too hard on herself. She had never actually seen a real deer, so maybe she hadn't done too bad a job after all!

Turning away from the sculpture, she made her way down to the water's edge and sat down on the damp sand, removing her handmade straw hat and sandals before wriggling her toes in the cool water. She leaned her head back, letting the last of the afternoon sunshine wash over her. It would soon be time to leave, and she relished the small amount of freedom she had here.

As she sat there, she was vaguely aware of the stillness of the afternoon air being broken by the sound of splashing water, and her head lolled forward, her eyes searching out the noise. Squinting, she made out a dark shape in the dark-blue waters, and for a moment she thought it was a dolphin, but as she focused on the shape she realised that it wasn't a dolphin but a man swimming, a very powerful swimmer, she thought, as she watched him cleave his way through the water, his arms strong and measured as they cut through the waves.

He was a very good. Maybe he was in training for some upcoming games? Perhaps the celebration of the birthday of the late Emperor Augustus next week she mused to herself. But her thoughts were cut short abruptly, and she tensed, drawing her knees up to her chest, when she realised that the swimmer had changed direction and was swimming straight towards her!

Not sure what to do, she stood up and watched the approaching figure, every sense she possessed on alert. Then, making up her mind, she turned abruptly and started to walk away.

"Wait! Please. I won't hurt you."

His words, spoken directly behind, sounded as if he was slightly out of breath and Justina stopped short. For a moment she hesitated, undecided what to do. *How had he got to the beach so quickly?* She thought in amazement. She turned around slowly, and when she saw him she swallowed the lump in her throat as she stared open-mouthed at the young man who had called out to her and who was now walking slowly towards her. The intensity of his eyes on hers was disconcerting, and she quickly looked away. But then, as if he had some sort of hold over her, she looked back up at him.

He looked like a young Neptune, rising from the waves, as he came out of the water towards her. He was naked apart from his *subligaculum.* The leather loin cloth moulded his hips snugly, and Justina's eyes looked away from there, quickly shifting to his muscular bronzed torso. His chest was hard and smooth, and she had the strange urge to stroke her hands over it to see if it was as strong and powerful as it looked.

Her artist's eye took in the perfect proportions of his body. His long muscular legs, narrow hips, his flat stomach, then up once more to his chest, and then finally, her wide-eyed gaze settled on his broad shoulders. She had to acknowledge that he was a perfect specimen of manhood, and secretly her hands itched to sculpt him, to feel his muscles, to—

"My name is Marsallas."

The words were spoken softly, and effectively acted as a splash of cold water to Justina's wayward thoughts. Instantly, her eyes shot up and met his twinkling blue ones. Realising that she had been caught staring at him, she blushed bright red when she saw the humour reflected in his gaze. Mortification surged through and she turned away from him.

Oh no, how could she have been so blatant? What must he think of her?

She turned slightly and looked at him from under her lashes. She could see that he was standing there staring at her, waiting for her to say something. "Justina," she finally said, aware of the huskiness of her voice. "My name is Justina."

Marsallas nodded slowly and smiled at her, his perfect, straight teeth a startling white against the bronze of his skin.

"Hello, Justina. Will you sit with me?"

She hesitated, aware of her hands twisting together nervously, "I…I…"

He must had sensed her hesitation, because he said quietly, "You are a very good sculptress by the way," he said nodding at the sand sculpture next to her. "Please. Stay for a little while," he begged.

Justina glanced up at him, chewing her bottom lip in indecision. She really should leave. The day was growing late and her father would expect her back soon. But seeing the earnest expression in his deep-blue eyes she made up her mind to stay. So she nodded slightly and noted in surprise that his shoulders slumped, as a look of relief passed over his face when she accepted his request.

"How old are you?" Marsallas asked, once she had sat back down on the sand and he had joined her.

Justina was slightly taken aback by the question, "Fifteen," she answered slowly, and when she saw him frown, she added, "But I'll be sixteen next month."

"So young," Marsallas said, almost to himself.

"And you? How old are you?" She murmured, noticing the husky edge to her voice once more.

"Eighteen."

"So old!" She said, her tone gently teasing.

Marsallas smiled at her, and grunted softly before he raised a mocking eyebrow at her in recognition of her answer. Justina couldn't help but smile back, and at that moment they both relaxed, as an understanding flowed between them. For the next hour they talked, tentatively at first, as strangers do when they first get to know each other, but after a while they talked easily, as if they had known each other for years, each of them sharing a little of themselves.

"My father is Aulus Justus Phillipus, he is the town's baker. Do you know him?"

Marsallas shook his head as a sudden bleakness washed over his face. "No I don't. Unfortunately, I don't get out much."

Justina looked up at him, as she noted the dark undertone in his voice when he said the last sentence.

"Oh. I…I see."

Marsallas smiled at her, his voice gentle, "I don't think you do, Justina. But it is of no consequence."

Not sure of what to say in response to that, she decided to change the subject. "Do you live nearby?"

"Umm. Over there," he said gesturing to his right, to where the large marble villas stretched along the shoreline of Herculaneum. Justina's eyes widened in surprise. She knew that the villas along the beach were owned by the *patricians*, the rich and elite of Herculaneum. *Just who was Marsallas, and why was he interested in her?* Then before she could stop herself she blurted out, "Are you a slave?"

Marsallas threw back his head and laughed for what seemed the longest time. Justina wondered why he found what she'd asked so amusing, and when he finally stopped and looked over to where she sat, he must have noticed the small frown of annoyance on her face, because he took pity on her and finally answered her. "No I am not a slave, Justina. Although I might as well be one."

Justina opened her mouth to ask why, but never had the chance to voice her question as Marsallas leaned forward and placed a finger on her lips. "No more questions, Justina. Please."

Seeing the pleading look on his face, Justina closed her mouth and turned away, shyness stealing through her.

Marsallas sighed, "Now I have upset you. I'm sorry."

Justina looked across at him, and shook her head, "No, it is I who should apologise. I had no right to pry."

She saw his eyes close and heard his soft groan of remorse, before he shifted closer to her. "You were not prying. It's…it's just that I find it so hard to share myself with anyone. I'm not used to having anyone care about me." Then he leaned forward and she watched mesmerised as his mouth came towards hers. Then his lips were on hers, and they both gasped in unison as a frisson of awareness surged through them both.

"Sweet. So sweet, as I knew you would be," Marsallas whispered, his breath mingling with hers as his fingers gently cupped the softness of her jaw, squeezing gently until Justina had no choice but to open her mouth. Her gasp of pleasure was obviously what he wanted to hear, as his tongue probed deeper, teasing and tasting the sweetness within. Then the kiss, gentle at first, changed, deepening in its intensity as Marsallas increased the pressure of his mouth on hers as he felt her passion match his.

Justina didn't know who pulled away first, but after what seemed like a lifetime their lips parted and they just stared at each other, young lovers caught up in the intensity of their first kiss, their first embrace. She shivered at the expression she saw in his blue eyes. Desire had darkened them to almost black, and she watched entranced unable, and unwilling, to look away.

It was Marsallas who ended their embrace, and Justina inwardly mourned the loss of his arms around her when he finally stood up.

"I have to go. Will you come tomorrow?" he asked quietly, staring down at her intently.

Justina nodded. "I'll try. It depends on my father and whether he will go to—" She stopped speaking abruptly, unwilling to say any more, but not before she saw the small frown that creased his brow.

"Like I said earlier, Justina. We all have things we want to keep to ourselves," he murmured after an awkward silence had fallen between them. His tone was gentle, soothing, as if he understood her plight, her reluctance to tell him everything.

"Yes. I…I…"

"Try to come tomorrow if you can," he said, interrupting her faltering words as he smiled down at her, in what was an obvious attempt to lighten the tension between them. "It is important that you do, as we have unfinished business."

Justina looked up at him in surprise. "Unfinished business? What unfinished business?"

Marsallas grinned wickedly, "Why, the business of getting to know each other, of course. Farewell, my beautiful Justina."

Then before she could say another word, he turned and ran back towards the water edge and waded out into the cold water before swimming away, leaving Justina staring after him.

* * *

"Lie still please! I've nearly finished."

"How can I? With a million ants crawling over me. I'm sure one has just crawled up my ar- err – up crevices I never knew I had."

"Marsallas!" She cried, her tone horrified.

Marsallas laughed. "You are such an innocent!"

"Stop teasing," she said, smiling at him. "Please Marsallas, just a few minutes more. I promise."

She heard him grunt, the noise conveying to Justina that he didn't believe her for one moment, and she couldn't contain her giggle. But he obeyed her plea, and she saw him assume the position she wanted, his body unnaturally still.

"Is this pose really necessary? My poor legs and arms are killing me. I must look stupid."

"Yes, the pose is necessary. You are supposed to be Jupiter defending the Empire, about to jump a hurdle. Now be quiet." Inwardly she laughed, but said nothing more. She saw him move his head slightly, knowing that he was watching her, and a glow of pleasure went through her as she felt the heat of his gaze on her.

But then her work took over and a frown of concentration settled on her brow as she knelt on the sand, her hands quick and frantic as they moulded and shaped the damp sand. It was over an hour later when she finally stood up. "There, I have finished. You can get up now."

"At last!" Marsallas said, groaning theatrically, as he rose from where he had been lying, busily brushing the sand off his body.

He walked over to where Justina stood next to the sand sculpture and glanced down at it. He let out a gasp of surprise and looked up at her, stunned amazement on his face. "It…it is wonderful! Unbelievable."

She blushed and glanced away in embarrassment. "Really?" She breathed, as if she could not quite believe what he said, as if she could not see her own genius.

"Yes, really. You have a brilliant talent. It is as if the sand is about to fly off into the air, it is so lifelike."

Justina smiled up at him and he smiled back, their eyes locked. Then Justina pushed him away gently, breaking the spell, "Go and wash yourself, you are covered in sand – and ants!"

Later they sat by the water's edge, the waves of the sea lapping gently at their feet as they watched the setting sun. They both knew that the time was approaching when they would have to leave.

"Is there no way you can start sculpturing properly? You have such talent it is a waste to see your sculptures washed away by the incoming tide."

Justina smiled sadly. "My father is only a poor baker. He – *we* – work incredibly hard. There is not much money left over for luxuries such as letting me train as a sculptress. Besides, it is a male dominated world, I doubt very much whether anyone would take me on as an apprentice."

"But—"

Marsallas stopped short, but she knew what he was going to say. They'd had this conversation before, on quite a few occasions in fact, during the past few weeks of their acquaintance. He was going to argue the point that surely her father made a decent enough living as the town's best baker, to afford to let her train as a sculptress.

But thankfully, this time he said nothing. Instead, she saw him lean over and rummage in a small cloth sack he had brought with him.

"I nearly forgot," he said, taking out a small wooden box and handing it over to her, murmuring softly, "Happy birthday, Justina."

Her eyes shot to meet his sparkling blue ones, "You remembered!" she exclaimed, as she took the small box, her hands trembling.

"Of course I remembered. It's not every day a girl has her sixteenth birthday."

"What is it?" She asked, looking down at the small wooden box she held in her open palm.

Marsallas smiled, "Why don't you open it and find out."

Justina looked down at the box, then back up at Marsallas. She smiled, a radiant smile that lit up her face. Then she looked down and carefully opened the box, unable to contain her gasp of shock when she saw the ring inside. Hesitantly she took it out and stared entranced at the beautiful gold and ruby ring that sparkled in the late-afternoon sunshine.

"It was my mother's. Do you like it?"

She knew how much he had loved his mother, and how he had been devastated when she had died when he was just ten years old. So giving her a ring that must have been so precious to him, seemed to forge the bond between them even closer. Even more so, as Marsallas knew that Justina, too, had lost her mother when she was only a baby.

Now as she lifted tear-filled eyes to his, she breathed, "Oh Marsallas, it is beautiful. I have never seen anything so lovely." Then she frowned and shook her head slightly. "But this is too precious to give to me. It was your mother's. Are you sure? I mean—"

"Justina. It's yours," he said interrupting her, his tone firm but gentle. "My mother would have loved you. She would have been proud for you to have it. Truly."

The tears Justina had been trying to hold back fell, and Marsallas groaned, pulling her into his arms, "Don't cry. Please."

"I am crying with happiness, Marsallas." Justina hiccupped, "Thank you so much, I will treasure this always," she said placing the ring on her middle finger, before she looked up at him.

Marsallas smiled down at her, but then his smiled faded, as he leaned forward and kissed her passionately. Eventually they pulled away to stare at each other and Marsallas whispered, "I love you, Justina."

Justina smiled up at him, her eyes shining with unshed tears, "And I love you as well Marsallas, with all my heart."

Marsallas groaned again, and pulled her back into his arms. Without conscious thought Justina's arms wound around his neck, and they kissed with such passion, such longing that neither of them heard the man approaching until it was too late.

"Justina! What in the name of Jupiter are you doing, girl?" The booming voice directly behind her registered immediately, but before she could react, she was wrenched unceremoniously away from Marsallas with such force that she gasped in pain.

"Father!" Justina moaned, staring up in disbelief at the angry man who loomed over her, and Marsallas, his hand clamped like a vice around the softness of her upper arm as he pulled her away from Marsallas.

"But I don't understand, father? Where are we going?" Justina cried, moments later as her father dragged her away from Marsallas. She saw through pain-filled eyes that Marsallas was being restrained by a giant of a man – a slave most probably – as he tried to wrestle free from his grip and come to her defence.

"Marsallas!" Justina cried, seeing the desperation on his face as he struggled ineffectually to get away.

Justina was aware that she was being taken, not to their home in the centre of the town, but along a path to a large marble villa.

"Quiet girl," her father growled, shaking her as she struggled once again, and Justina, afraid by the anger that had consumed her father, stopped her struggling and said nothing until eventually they reached the gate of an imposing villa. As if they were expected, the gates swung open, and they were met by a silent slave who led them into the opulent villa, through magnificent high-ceiling rooms, until they were finally left alone in the *tablinum*. Justina turned to her father, begging him for an explanation, but he had remained mute, refusing to answer her questions, his face pale and his hands shaking.

Eventually, after what had seemed like a lifetime, the door had opened and a man of around fifty entered the room. He was tall and thin, and wore a toga of the finest linen.

Justina knew instantly who it was. Marsallas's uncle. Quintus.

Even if Marsallas had not described him, she would have known who he was. Quintus was his uncle on his father's side and she could see the family resemblance. Like Marsallas he had piercing blue eyes – but his were as cold as ice – and she couldn't control the shiver of fear that went through her as he stared at her.

"Have you told her?" He asked her father, never once taking

his eyes off Justina. Justina saw her father shake his head, sweat popping out on his forehead. "No."

"Good." Then saying nothing more, Quintus arranged his toga before he sat down on one of the luxuriously covered chairs. Taking some grapes from a golden platter, he waved his hand for them both to sit down.

Justina's father sat down heavily in another chair, and Justina realising that she didn't have much choice, slowly sat down next to him.

"I can see why my nephew is besotted with you. You are very beautiful. Come over here and sit beside me."

Justina blanched at his words, and looked across at her father, "Father, please—"

"Cease!" Quintus shouted at her, before he swivelled his eyes to her father and bit out, "You should keep your daughter under control, man. She has too much freedom, too much tongue in her head. Now I said come over here."

The colour drained from her face as Justina realised that her father seemed powerless to protect her, and reluctantly she rose and went over to sit next to Quintus. A shiver of revulsion coursed through her when he took her hand in his, his cold, thin fingers rubbing the softness of her palm. Glancing over to where her father sat, Justina saw his shoulders slump in defeat, totally crushed by whatever hold this man had over him.

Once Quintus was sure that he had the upper hand once more, he continued speaking, his voice matter of fact and totally imper-sonal. "Your father is in a lot of trouble, Justina. He owes me a tremendous amount of money. His gambling has got out of control I'm afraid."

At his words, Justina glanced sharply across at her father, desperate for him to deny what the older man was saying. But when she saw her father's face visibly age in front of her, she couldn't help the feeling of sickness that assailed her, "No." She whispered, her head shaking from side to side, refusing to believe what she was hearing.

Looking up at her, his face as pale as death, her father whispered, "I am sorry child. Truly sorry."

"But father. We can work it out. We did it before. We can do it again," desperation edged her voice as she pleaded with him.

Quintus's fingers dug into the softness of her skin, and Justina winced in pain as she was forced to look back at him.

"How noble. How brave," Quintus mocked, "But I'm afraid your father has got in too deep this time. He owes me a lot of money – money that has to be repaid now!"

"But I don't understand—"

Quintus slammed his other fist down on a table that stood next to him, the action causing both Justina and her father to jump in fright. "I won't tell you again, girl. You talk too much. As my mistress you will learn your place. You will learn to be seen and not heard!"

Justina took a deep, shuddering breath at his words, unable for a moment to take in what he said. "Mistress?" She finally whispered, "I...I don't understand?"

Quintus sighed dramatically, a bored look on his face. "Do I have to spell it out for you girl? I thought it would be obvious. Your father has bartered you – given you to me – to pay off his debts."

"No! No it is impossible, I love Marsallas—"

"Marsallas!" Quintus spat, shaking her like one of the straw dolls she used to play with as a child. "I don't think so my dear. You will be mine, not Marsallas's. And if you tell him anything of this, I will crush you and your father, *and* I will crush Marsallas. I will make Marsallas's life a living death, so much so that he will wish he is in Hades if you say one word to him of this. Do you understand me?"

Justina said nothing, her face deathly pale. She knew in that instant – that moment – as she glanced over to where her father sat, crushed and defeated, his head bent with the weight of his sorrow, that her life was about to change forever.

Looking away from her father, she saw Quintus's lips curl in disgust at her father's weakness, and she shivered in trepidation as she recalled everything that Marsallas had told her about his uncle. His cruelty. His anger. His brutality. The callous way he treated everybody.

Even his only wife hadn't escaped his tyranny. She had died a broken woman, a mere shadow of the vibrant person she had once been, according to Marsallas. And now it seemed that neither she nor her father would escape either.

It was, as if by some cruel twist of fate, that she had just become the main prize in some obscure contest between uncle and nephew, and now between Quintus and her father.

And then, as if things couldn't have gotten any worse, the door to the *tablinum* had flown open and Marsallas had barged in, a furious look on his face as he took in the scene before him. It was obvious he had managed to escape from the slave, because the slave ran into the room moments later and grabbed him by his arms, restraining him once more, when Marsallas had come to an abrupt halt inside the room.

"What in Jupiter's name is going on?" he shouted, trying to wrestle out of the slave's clutches, but his fight was futile as the slave's size and strength was so very much greater than his, and after a few moments he stopped in his attempts to free himself.

Quintus, confident now that his nephew was no threat to him, smiled over to him, "Ahh, Marsallas, I am glad you are here. You are just in time to congratulate me," his tone was sarcastic. Then he raised his hand – the same hand that held Justina's – up in the air.

Marsallas stiffened, and his eyes narrowed when he saw their clasped hands, but refusing to be baited he remained mute.

"Nothing to say, boy? Well I'll tell you then, shall I? Justina has just agreed to be my mistress. She has been a bit remiss in not telling you what's been going on, so I thought it was about time that you found out."

A stunned silence fell in the room once Quintus had stopped

speaking.

For what seemed like aeons, but in actuality was only seconds, Marsallas glared at his uncle before he finally broke eye contact and looked at Justina.

"Tell me it is not true, Justina?" He whispered, his eyes pleading, begging her to deny what his uncle spoke.

Justina bit back the tears that threatened to fall when she saw the pained expression on his face, physically swallowing the lump of emotion that threatened to choke the very life out of her. Breaking eye contact with him, she turned slightly to look at Quintus, seeing in that instant the evil radiating out of him, the madness in his eyes, as he seemed to relish the misery he was inflicting on the three people in the room with him.

She knew with a certainty that Quintus was capable of destroying them all if she didn't acquiesce to his demands. He would crush each and every one of them without a moment's hesitation, if she denied anything he'd said.

So she turned, her face as pale as death, and her heart breaking into a thousand pieces, and said, "I'm sorry Marsallas. I—"

"You said you loved *me* Justina, only me," he interjected, his face draining of colour as the enormity of what she was telling him sank in. And when she said nothing in her defence she saw him stiffen.

"All this time you were planning to be my uncle's *mistress*?" Disgust replaced shock and she saw his fists clench and unclench in rage, before he spat, "May you rot in Hades, Justina. I hope you remember me every night, whilst you lie on your back with your legs spread for *him*!"

And with that, he wrestled out of the slave's grip, and the slave realising he was no longer a threat, had let him go.

* * *

The light touch on her arm jolted her back to the present. Eyes focusing, she looked up at Diogenes, the same slave who had restrained Marsallas all those years ago on that fateful night.

"What?" Then she looked around her, surprised to see that the crowds were rapidly dispersing, the games finally over for the day. She shook her head slightly, "I'm sorry, Diogenes. I was far away."

Then, without another word, she stood up and followed the crowds out of the arena, leaving behind her past once more, her heart heavy and sad.

CHAPTER FOUR

"I'm sorry, Justina. There is nothing more I can do. I've made him as comfortable as possible." Lydia said, as Justina entered the darkened bed chamber.

Justina nodded as she walked over to where Lydia, her friend and a well-respected healer, stood. "I understand, Lydia. Thank you for all your help."

She spoke the words softly and Lydia smiled at her, placing a hand on the younger woman's arm in a gesture of comfort, as Justina looked down at Quintus, who lay as still as death on his large bed.

"It is the least I could do. Do you need anything? A sleeping draught or something?"

Justina shook her head, "No, I will be fine. Thank you."

Lydia said nothing more, but squeezed the younger woman's arm in understanding before she left the room, closing the door with a soft click behind her. The finality of it caused Justina to shiver, her eyes automatically glancing over to a table along the back wall, seeing the wax death mask displayed so prominently. It had arrived that afternoon, rather appropriately she thought, as it now acted as a constant reminder of Quintus's imminent death.

Looking away from the mask, she stared down at Quintus. He looked so still, as if he were already dead. The sunken hollows under his razor-sharp cheekbones were so pronounced that no flesh remained on his face – or the rest of his body for that matter – and the blue veins on his hands stood out in stark contrast to the whiteness of his parchment-thin skin. But she saw his chest move in small shaky movements, testament that he still clung to life, refusing to die, refusing to succumb to the disease that had been eating away at him for months now.

Justina sighed, and turned away, looking up at the man who stood silently next to his master. "You can leave if you want, Diogenes. There is nothing more anyone can do."

Justina didn't expect a reply from the slave – he was a man of few words. But he didn't leave and Justina shivered, ever so slightly in awe of the slave, even after all these years. She remembered the first time she had seen him, the feeling of shock that had assailed her as he loomed over her, black fathomless eyes staring down at her from a body nearly seven feet in height, and this, coupled with his massive strength – his chest alone was the size of three men's – had rendered her immobile with fright.

His skin was as dark as mahogany and his bald oiled head, complete with earring, made him look like some giant pirate, but Justina knew that he had been captured many years ago as a young boy from Syria. She couldn't tell how old he was, he seemed ageless somehow, but she knew that he must be at least forty years old by now—

A loud groan interrupted her thoughts and she looked down at Quintus, surprised to see that he was awake for the first time since she had come back from Rome. Justina leaned over and laid her hand on the cold skin of his forehead. "Shh, Quintus. Rest now."

Quintus shook his head and lifted a finger towards Diogenes, beckoning the slave forward. Once the slave had approached, Quintus rasped, "Lift me."

"No Quintus, you must lie still," she implored, a frown of concern on her face.

But Quintus ignored her, waving her away, and Diogenes, as

ordered by his master, lifted the old man until he was upright, and placed a silk cushion behind his back. For several moments Quintus gasped for breath, the exertion causing him serious distress.

Eventually Quintus's breathing steadied, and once he was able to breathe normally he looked over to Diogenes. "Leave," he ordered.

Justina watched as the slave left the room, then she tensed when she saw his gaze come to rest on hers, a hard look in his eyes. She had seen that look many times over the past six years, and knew that it boded ill. Quintus beckoned her over and Justina, not having much choice, walked over to stand by his bed. He took her hand, his bony fingers gripping the softness of hers. "Did you see him? As I ordered you too?"

Justina stiffened, before she answered, "Yes."

"And?"

"He won't come."

The three words held a wealth of meaning and Quintus cackled. "Of course he won't." He breathed hard, before he rasped, "And how was he?"

Justina frowned, not sure what he wanted her to say. But she spoke the truth anyway. "Hard. Indomitable. Full of hate."

A cruel smile touched his lips, "Good. It was about time he became a man instead of fawning over you. What else?"

The question was fired rapidly and Justina flinched slightly, "He said his life in Herculaneum was over, and he had no desire to return."

"Not even for you?"

The question caused Justina's heart to race, and she suddenly felt faint. Lifting her chin in defiance she fixed her gaze on his, refusing to be cowed. "No. Not even for me."

Quintus's eyes narrowed, the blue of his eyes like shards of ice, "Are you sure of that, Justina? He couldn't keep his hands off you when he was younger."

Justina sucked in her breath, refusing to answer his question.

Instead she asked her own, "Why are you so full of hatred, Quintus?" Her voice was low, measured, with the depth of the emotion she was feeling, "Can't you just leave it be? You know what you did tore us apart; can never be repaired. Be content with *that* as you lie here on your death bed."

And with that she turned to leave, but his words halted her, causing a trickle of fear to course through her.

"I wouldn't be too sure of that, Justina. I've sown the seeds of hate once again," he said cryptically.

Closing the door to Quintus's bedroom, Justina made her way down the dark corridor, her brow furrowed as she thought of Quintus's words. He was so bitter. So full of hatred. Even now, with his death imminent, he still festered a hatred for his nephew that defied logic.

Deep in thought, she was unprepared for the shadow that suddenly came to life from behind one of the marble columns. She stiffened, instantly on the defensive, thinking it was Secundus.

But it wasn't Secundus, and Justina felt her heart lurch in surprise when she saw Marsallas standing there.

Had it been five whole days since she'd seen last seen him? It seemed like a lifetime ago. Her stomach muscles contracted as she took in a deep breath, watching as he came towards her, his eyes burning into hers so intensely that she didn't know whether to run away from him or run into his arms, such were the myriad feelings running through her head.

She did neither. Instead she merely stood her ground. A shiver ran through her, trickling down her spine like ice-cold mountain water. Eventually she found her tongue and silently cursed the husky tone of her voice as she said, "You have come."

The words once blurted out now sounded stupid and she blushed in mortification. It didn't help when she saw Marsallas's mouth quirk in a slight smile at her gaucheness.

"So I have."

Those three words held a wealth of meaning, and Justina looked away as an awkward silence fell between them.

"Is Quintus in there?"

Turning her head back to him, she became aware that he had moved closer to her and her lips were now no more than a whisper away from his. Her stomach plummeted as she fought the urge to fuse her lips with his. To taste him. All of him.

"Yes," she finally answered.

"Can I see him?"

Justina nodded. "He was still awake when I just left." For a moment she wondered whether she should mention the conversation that had just taken place. Making up her mind quickly, she blurted out, "He wasn't in a very good mood, I'm afraid. He was questioning me about you…"

Her words trailed off. For a long moment Marsallas said nothing, just stared down at her, his eyes expressionless. Then he walked past her and stopped in front of the door, before he turned to where Justina was still standing, "Will you come in with me?"

For a moment she hesitated, unsure. But then she saw a glimpse of uncertainty – fleeting – but none the less there – enter his eyes before it was blinked away. "Yes. Of course," she said, making up her mind.

* * *

"Quintus? Marsallas is here," Justina whispered, unsure whether he was asleep or not, as his eyes were now closed. For a few moments silence reigned in the room until Quintus's eyes suddenly shot open, causing Justina to jump slightly with the unexpectedness of it. His eyes bored into hers briefly, before they swivelled to where Marsallas stood on the other side of the bed.

For an indeterminably long time both men stared at each other, each of them taking the other's measure.

Considering how ill Quintus was, Justina was surprised to see anger and hatred radiating out of Quintus's eyes, before his lips, parchment-thin, curled in disgust as he looked his nephew up and down.

Eventually Quintus spoke, "Well, what a surprise. My long-lost nephew returns at last."

Justina held her breath, amazed by the vitriol she could hear in Quintus's voice, and she glanced over to Marsallas awaiting his response.

"Uncle," Marsallas nodded in greeting, his tone neutral. But the word held a wealth of feeling, and Justina ached with pity for him. Inwardly she was annoyed with Quintus. Hadn't Marsallas come to see him, as ordered? And now that he had, Quintus was *still* angry with him! It seemed that nothing Marsallas could do would ever please his uncle.

"She's still beautiful isn't she? I can see why you lusted over her."

The words made Justina stiffen in shock, totally unprepared by Quintus's line of attack. What on earth was he playing at? Looking down at him, she saw a twisted smile on the old man's face, as he stared intently at his nephew.

Marsallas said nothing, but Justina could feel the tension flowing between the two of them, like two adversaries about to commence battle in the gladiatorial arena. Nerves pooled in her stomach as she glanced at Marsallas from under her lashes. If Marsallas was of a mind, he could quite easily mention that he kissed her when she had seen him in Rome. That would be enough to rile his uncle's anger, she was sure of it!

Thankfully, Marsallas never responded to his uncle's jibe, but Justina could tell that the words had affected him, as a nerve ticked furiously along his clenched jawline.

"Take her if you want. I've no use for her any more!"

Justina gasped, suddenly feeling faint, her hand reaching out to the wall to steady herself. "Why Quintus?" she cried out, unable to look at Marsallas because of the shame that filled her. And when Quintus didn't even bother to look at her, never mind answer her, she turned and fled the room, unable to stop the tears that fell.

The silence in the room was deafening once the door had slammed shut behind Justina, and unable to control his temper, Marsallas leaned forward, his lips curling with disgust.

"Once a bastard, always a bastard, eh uncle?" Marsallas's lips curled in disgust, "And for a moment I thought you might have changed, shown some compassion as you lay here on your death bed."

Quintus stared up at his nephew, his eyes full of hatred, and with a huge effort he raised a bony finger, pointing it at him, "Why should I change, Marsallas? I've no need to change. You'll do well to remember that, *especially* when you take Justina to your bed. And you will—" he said, pausing, spittle dribbling down his chin, as he saw confusion flit across Marsallas's face. Then, slowly, deliberately, and for maximum effect he added, "But don't forget, *I* had her first!"

CHAPTER FIVE

Justina woke up with a start, wondering what had disturbed her. Then her ears attuned to the strange sounds coming from outside the villa, and she sat up, swinging her legs out of the bed before walking over to the window.

As she looked down into the courtyard she saw a myriad musicians testing their instruments, and paid wailers warming up their vocal cords to the requisite pitch of grief. Her eyes took in the macabre sight of dancers practising their moves, and actors running through their last rehearsals of the tricks and idiosyncrasies of the family ancestors whom they were to impersonate.

Normally, the villa was quiet in the mornings, Quintus had demanded that there should be no noise whatsoever until he had awoken.

But Quintus was dead, and for five days now there had been a surreal atmosphere in the villa. The death of such a prominent man as Quintus demanded a high-profile funeral, and ever since the morning of his death, when the funeral director had arrived and promptly closed the heavy doors of the villa before nailing bushy sprigs of pine to it, to declare the presence of the dead within, there had been a flurry of activity everywhere.

As if by magic, musicians had arrived soon after, and mournful music filled the scented gloom of the *atrium*, where the floor was piled with baskets of fruit and wreathes of flowers in homage. The funeral director had then ordered his men to arrange the decorative tributes around the couch on which the dead man rested, before opening a series of cupboards to reveal the yellow-skinned wax death masks.

Today was the day of the funeral, and hopefully, afterwards, everything would return to some sort of normality – whatever that would be! Nothing seemed real any more. She felt as if she were suspended in time, waiting for something to happen.

Sighing, she turned away from the chaos outside and started to dress, not bothering to wait for her tire-woman to attend to her. In truth, she wanted to crawl back under the silk covers and hide for ever, avoid the funeral and everything that came with it. But she couldn't. Duty called. *Everyone* expected the former lover of one of Herculaneum's richest men to be present at his funeral…

* * *

Later that morning, as the funeral cortège left the villa, the first thing the people of Herculaneum saw, as the huge gates of the villa were opened, was an actor wearing the wax death mask and accompanying Quintus's corpse as it was carried on a large litter on his last journey. Custom dictated that the body be exposed to view for the duration of the procession, formally dressed and arranged by the undertaker, and Justina watched in morbid fascination as Quintus's body swayed, almost lifelike, in the cart in front of her, as she and Lydia followed behind it.

Justina knew no expense had been spared for Quintus's funeral. Two thousand *sesterces* had been donated towards the perfumes alone, almost all of which would go up to the heavens in sweet smoke by the time the ninth day of mourning was over.

Tearing her eyes away from the dead body, Justina looked ahead of her, hearing the muted whispers of the crowds that lined the cobbled, narrow streets as they slowly made their way into the centre of Herculaneum. As she sidestepped puddles of rain that had fallen the night before, she could see that they were approaching the Forum, noticing that it was freshly festooned with garlands of flowers for a forthcoming festival.

The Forum was an almost exact copy of the Forum found in Rome, albeit smaller, and for a heartbeat she remembered the brief time she had spent there. Remembered Marsallas's kisses, his hands on her body, and the heat in his eyes when he looked at her, before hate had replaced desire—

"Are you all right Justina?"

Justina started, her memories disappearing in an instant as she turned to look at Lydia, who walked next to her. She smiled to herself at the concern she could hear in her friend's voice, before giving the older woman a brief nod, "Yes, I think so. But I'm attracting a lot of attention, though," she said quietly, as she saw that the crowd were either watching her or whispering about her. Justina knew it wouldn't be until the wax masks had been returned to their cupboards, the family had been purged with fire and water, and the house finally swept and purified with roasted salt and spelt, that she would finally be free of the covert looks and judgement that had followed her the moment she had left the confines of the villa.

Lydia smiled at the younger woman, before saying drolly, "Well, it's not surprising really, this is the first time the *plebeians* of Herculaneum have ever seen the mistress of the mighty Aulus Epidius Quintus," then, her voice hardening slightly she continued, "Because for six years he has practically kept you a prisoner in that villa!"

Justina said nothing when she heard the anger in Lydia's voice, for there was nothing she could say. Lydia spoke the truth. Quintus *had* kept her hidden away from the outside world, and she could count on one hand the number of times that she had been allowed to leave the villa, and only then when he had allowed it. When she had first arrived at the villa, she had begged Quintus to let her lead a normal life, to leave the confines of the villa to do normal things, like shop or go to the baths. But he had refused point-blank and had then forbidden her to ask him any more, warning her that she would be punished if she did so.

Finally, they came to the entrance of the Forum, and as the eulogy started, a hush descended over the crowd. The impersonated actors stopped their tomfoolery and sat motionless in their ivory *curule* chairs, and as she stood listening to the magistrate's long speech she glanced across at Lydia, who stood next to her, thankful for all the help she, and her husband Marcus, and the rest of their family had given her these past few days. She knew with a certainty that without them she wouldn't have been able to cope.

Over an hour later the magistrate finally finished his eulogy, and Justina breathed a silent prayer of relief. The funeral was nearly over, and as she turned to walk behind the cortège, her manner dignified, she surveyed the crowd, noticing with a slight blush of embarrassment, that she was still being watched by most of them.

And then she saw him, leaning against one of the marble columns of the *basilica*.

Marsallas! So he had come to the funeral after all.

Her stomach fluttered, when she saw with a hint of trepidation, that he was watching her intently. She could feel the colour draining from her face, but she refused to be cowed, refused to succumb to the power that radiated from him. For a moment she wondered what on earth had persuaded him to turn up here. He didn't have any reason to be here. After all, there had been no love between him and his uncle. And even though he was some twenty feet away from her, she could feel the heat of his gaze, as if it were reaching across the crowd towards her. Hot, raw and sensual, it pierced right to the core of her body, and she shivered at the feelings that assailed her, unable to tear her eyes from his. Heat curled in her stomach, as a wave of pure longing surged through her.

Then he smiled across at her, a smile that never reached his eyes, mocking her, tormenting her, as if he knew *exactly* what she was thinking, what she was feeling.

Tearing her gaze away from his, she stared down at the cobbled pavement, concentrating on placing one foot in front of the other.

"It's nearly over, Justina. We will soon be at the villa."

Lydia's words broke into her tormented thoughts, and she looked up, noticing in astonishment that the crowds were already drifting away. Quickly, she risked a glance over her shoulder, to where Marsallas had stood, but with a small jolt of regret saw that he wasn't there any more.

Sighing, she turned and followed Lydia as they made their way through the villa gates. Now all she had to do was survive the feast of remembrance that had been prepared at the villa, and then wait for the contents of Quintus's will to be read out. Some of the magistrates present at the funeral this morning had been appointed as executors of Quintus's will, and they had already informed her that it would be read out once the feast had been concluded.

Justina rubbed the dull ache at the back of her neck, as tension pooled there. Today was going to be long. Very long indeed…

* * *

"…To my faithful slave, Diogenes I give *manumission* and a stipend of one thousand *sesterces*."

Justina glanced up from where she sat, and looked across the room to where Diogenes stood. As usual the slave showed no emotion at the news that he had just been given his freedom, and she smiled to herself, wondering what he would do now that he was a free man at last.

Then she turned her attention back to the magistrate, who was reading out Quintus's will. So far it had been predictably long and boring, as Quintus thanked all those influential persons in Herculaneum for their support over the past years, but now, finally, it was getting to the important parts.

"I have sent a messenger to request Marsallas's presence here, as he—"

No sooner had the magistrate spoken, when the door opened, and Marsallas walked in. Justina felt her stomach drop, a slow warmth spreading through her. She watched as he closed the door behind him, leaning against the wooden door, his arms crossed in a gesture that brooked no resistance. He nodded at the magistrate who, like the rest of them had stopped dead in their tracks when he had entered the room.

The magistrate cleared his throat and continued, "Ahh, Marsallas. Good. Good. You have arrived. Now I can carry on with reading the rest of your uncle's will. It, rather coincidentally, concerns you," the magistrate drew in a deep breath and continued, "Your uncle has left all his goods and chattels, including his business interests, and this villa, to you his nephew, Aulus Epidius Marsallas."

At his words a collective gasp echoed around the quietness of the room, and Justina, like the others, could not contain her shock at what she was hearing.

Everything to Marsallas! But why? Everyone knew that Marsallas had been cut out of his uncle's will the day he ran away. Now, why after all these years had Quintus changed it? Justina rubbed her forehead in confusion, a headache starting behind her eyes. It didn't make any sense!

"Unfortunately, that is all there is in the will."

The magistrate's words brought Justina back to the present with a jolt, and she looked up to see the small smile of regret that he gave to her. Then the silence of the room was broken by the slamming of the door; and without having to look behind her she knew that Marsallas had left.

"He left you nothing. It is not right."

Justina turned to face Lydia. "I wouldn't have taken anything anyway."

"Yes, but—"

"It doesn't matter, Lydia. Truly. I didn't expect anything. I'm just surprised that Quintus gave everything to Marsallas, and not to his adopted son, Cnaeus."

Lydia nodded, silently agreeing with her, for it had been common knowledge for several years now, ever since Quintus had adopted Cnaeus, an adult son of one of the poorer merchants in the town, that he would inherit the bulk of Quintus's fortune.

"Justina, you do know you can always come and live with us. Our home is always open to you."

Justina felt tears spring in her eyes at her friend's words, seeing the earnest expression on her face.

"Oh, Lydia. You have all been so kind to me. I don't know what I would have done without you these past few years. I have been truly blessed to call you my friend."

Lydia opened her mouth to speak, but Justina continued, "But truthfully, I'm not sure what I want to do at the moment. As you know I have some money of my own. I need to think carefully as to what to do with the rest of my life. But thank you."

Lydia nodded, "I understand, Justina. But I promise you one thing. I won't let you suffer any more. If...if things don't work out and I have to resort to kidnapping you I will! You *will* live in a household that loves you!"

CHAPTER SIX

"More wine, Master?"

Marsallas shook his head, and the slave bowed before leaving him alone in the *triclinium*. As he sipped the wine he shook his head slightly. *Master*. The word sounded strange. He had never envisaged that he would ever come back to this place. He had vowed to himself when he had listened to his uncle's words on his deathbed that he would *never* set foot in this villa again.

So what went wrong? How on earth had he persuaded himself to return here? Not once, not twice, but three times! The second time had been on the day of Quintus's funeral, and the reading of his uncle's will, and now, the third time, some three days later.

He had gone back to Rome, the very afternoon he found out that his uncle had left him everything in his will, intending to appoint a lawyer to sell the villa and all his uncle's belongings, and donate all the proceeds to the poor of Rome.

But he hadn't. He'd barely lasted half a day there before he had returned, riding his horse hard, arriving here at his uncle's – his villa now – just over an hour ago. The villa had been in darkness, everyone had obviously retired, apart from the slave who manned the main gate. Once he had been let in, a sleepy slave had been summoned to provide him with refreshment, which he was now partaking of in the darkness of the *triclinium*.

Life had just got complicated all over again, he mused to himself. His life at the Circus Maximus was simple in many respects – it was just a matter of survival. Get in his chariot, race at breakneck speed around the arena, and hopefully live to tell the tale at the end of it. And if he was lucky, he would remain unscathed, win, and then take home the prize money.

He had a life outside the Circus of course – but many of his so-called friends knew nothing about this. It was his sanctuary from the madness of the Circus – a *villa rustica* – a massive self-supporting farm about two-hours ride out of Rome. But that was his secret life, and no one in the Circus, apart from a select few, knew about it.

For several more minutes Marsallas sat alone in the room, deep in thought. Then a wave of fatigue came over him. He was bone-tired, having ridden non-stop from Rome to get here, but he knew that he would not be able to sleep. His mind was whirling, his emotions in turmoil. Deciding he needed time to clear his head before he retired for the night, he took his drink and made his way out into the garden, before walking down to the pier and gazing out across the sea.

As he looked out across the Bay of Naples, the moonlight illuminating the inky blackness, he finally acknowledged to himself why he had come back to Herculaneum.

Justina. She was the reason. The *only* reason he was here. Ever since she had turned up at the Circus, she'd dominated his every waking thought. Once again she had gotten under his skin, and it was a feeling that left him totally unsettled.

He lifted his goblet and drowned the wine in one swallow, grimacing as the liquid burned down into his empty stomach. She was so beautiful, more so now, as the veneer of childhood had gone, to be replaced with full-blooded womanhood. Tall and slender, but with curves in all the right places. Her hair was as black as the night, long, swept back off her heart-shaped face, highlighting the high cheekbones and the soft fullness of her mouth. But it was her eyes that he was drawn, too. Eyes so dark, so passionate, he felt himself drowning in them. He remembered his hands, shaking with desire, sliding over the bareness of her sun-kissed skin all those years ago and he hungered to do it again.

And that was why he was here. The kisses they had shared at the Circus, and in the inn where she had stayed, had only whetted his appetite for more.

Yes, she was his dead uncle's mistress, but he still wanted her, still desired her. And *that*, as far as Marsallas was concerned was unfinished business.

Their unfinished business…

With a grim look on his face that boded ill for Justina, he turned from the pier and with purposeful strides walked back inside the villa. A few moments later he barged into his uncle's bedroom, only to stop dead in his tracks when he saw that the room was empty.

Totally empty. The large bed, a raised dais of massive proportions had been stripped of all its coverings, and the chest that would have held his uncle's belongings was open and empty. But more to the point, there was no sign of Justina.

Marsallas turned and walked back down the corridor. One, by one, he opened each of the doors to the other rooms in search of Justina, but she wasn't in any of them. Eventually he came to the last door. He hesitated for a moment before he opened it slowly and entered the room. Like a wolf stalking its prey, he made no noise as he walked over to the bed – what had once been *his* bed – and gazed down at Justina's sleeping figure. *What in Jupiter's name was she doing sleeping in his room?*

She slept on her side, a thin silk cover over her. He could make out her slim form as she slept under it, the light from the moon and the outside torches providing enough light to see her. Her knees were drawn up high to her chest and she had both of her hands tucked under her cheek. Her long black hair was unbound and streamed down her back, and she looked almost childlike as she lay there, her chest rising and falling with each breath she took.

He had never watched a woman sleep before, he realised with a start, as he stared down at her.

He had always left after having sex with the women he'd taken to his bed. He was blunt, to the point of rudeness, in stating his terms to any prospective lover at the outset of any new affair. And if that made him cold and hard in their eyes then so be it...

He knew why he did it, of course. It was his way of making sure no woman ever got under his skin. He avoided women who wanted "love". Lust was his only coin. The *only* way in which he conducted his affairs. The only way to ensure no woman *ever* took advantage of him or hurt him again...just as Justina had done...

But as he watched her sleep, he couldn't stop the pang of longing, the urge to lift the silken covers and lie next to her. And what? Hold her? Kiss her? Caress her? Take her...?

For several seconds he stared down at her, his brain racing furiously. Then she stirred, turning over onto her back, her hands lifting above her head and the silk sheet that had covered her from head to toe slipped down, revealing a tunic of white silk that moulded the softness of her curves.

His stomach tightened as his gaze lingered on her breasts, ripe and full, as they pushed against their silk covering. He fought the urge to lean forward, to kiss the silk, wet it with his mouth and see if her nipples reacted to his touch.

Had she learned how to please a man in his uncle's bed? His mouth twisted. He imagined she had. After all, Quintus had bedded her for six years. He swallowed hard as a metallic taste entered his mouth. He knew what it was. Jealousy. Bitterness. Raw anger.

It was what he had experienced six years ago when she had chosen his uncle instead of him. And now, after all these years it reared its ugly head once more. Had she lain with Quintus replete, sated from his lovemaking? He hoped not. But then he couldn't be too sure. Bedfellows came in all shapes and sizes. And money *always* had a way of sweetening the bitterness of choices poorly made.

He turned on his heel, stiff with anger that was evident in every line of his body and moved away from her to walk over to the open window. He stared sightlessly out of it, into the shadowed darkness beyond. It was the same window he'd looked out of as a teenager as he'd watched and waited for her to come to the beach. She would turn up, more or less at the same time every day, around the ninth hour, kneel down onto the sand and start to work furiously, moulding, shaping, creating magnificent sand sculptures for hours on end, only leaving when the sun set over the horizon.

His memories were interrupted when he heard a noise from across the room. Turning, he walked back to the bed, and saw that Justina was tossing and turning, a deep frown on her face. Her delicate scent, the merest hint of lavender, teased his nostrils and he felt his body harden. It was a scent unique to her, and it had driven him mad with longing when he was a youth.

He inhaled deeply, pulling the scent of her deep into his lungs, as he imagined her without clothing. Naked. Writhing beneath him, her back arched in wanton abandonment. The ultimate in temptation. And he wanted her. Desperately. She moaned something, and Marsallas leaned forward to try and make out what she was saying. But the words were incoherent and he realised that she was obviously distressed about something, and without conscious thought he leaned forward and shook her gently, waking her.

He saw her eyelashes flutter, and then her eyes opened, and for a heartbeat they remained unfocused, until the light from the moonlight illuminated his presence in the room, and she gasped in fright, pulling the thin silk cover up to her chin, the gesture one of pure protection. But then she must have realised who it was, as she whispered, "Marsallas! You have come back. I didn't think you would."

Marsallas said nothing. He watched her sit up slowly, using one arm to pull herself up, whilst with the other she gripped the silk cover in an age-old gesture of modesty. Her hair hung down her back in thick, black silken waves that shone as the moonlight reflected off them. Marsallas realised that this was the first time he had ever seen her hair unbound, and he had to resist the strong urge to wrap his fist in it and pull her forward, until—

"Is something wrong, Marsallas?" She asked, her voice hesitant.

Marsallas came back to earth with a start, and his eyes shot to hers. Eyes, he noticed, that were watching him intently. For a moment, neither of them moved as they stared at each other. Then he saw her tongue come out to moisten her lower lip, the movement so erotic that he found himself hardening with desire, and he moved towards her, placing his hands on either side of her headboard, trapping her. He leaned forward, inch by slow inch, until they were a hair's breath from touching each other, so close that Marsallas could see the pupils of hers eyes dilate in response to his nearness. They stared at each other. He could smell the sweet scent of her skin, lavender floating on a breeze, and he had to fight the urge to kiss her.

But then the sound of a screech from outside the window – an owl most probably – startled Justina, and the spell was broken between them. Marsallas pulled back from her as if he had suddenly been burnt.

He cursed himself for succumbing to her charms, and for nearly kissing her. Angry with himself for desiring her, wanting her so much, he lashed out, "Nothing is wrong, Justina. Nothing at all," he drawled, "I was wondering what you must have looked like in my uncle's bed every night, that is all. And now I know." His words caused her to gasp, and she recoiled from him, the desire he had seen in her huge grey eyes replaced by hurt.

"Get out!" She shouted, "Get out."

Marsallas hardened himself against the vulnerable picture she presented and bowed, the gesture a mocking one, his eyes unreadable as he looked down at her. "If you insist," and with that he left the room without a backward glance.

* * *

Justina only managed a few hours' sleep, having finally drifted off when the sun had started to rise. And when – her tire-woman – had come into the room barely an hour later she had risen listlessly before washing and donning a simple cotton *stola*. She now sat in a chair next to her bedroom table eating some fruit, as Olivia fussed about the room tidying it up. Once the young girl had finished, she set about styling Justina's hair. But unusually for her, Olivia was quiet, and concerned for her welfare, as normally the young girl was a little chatterbox, Justina asked, "All is well, Olivia?"

Olivia hesitated for a moment, her hand stilling momentarily as she brushed Justina's silken hair, before she answered, "I was wondering, Mistress, what will become of me, and the other slaves, now that the Master is dead."

Justina sighed, and she worried her bottom lip before replying, "In truth, I do not know, Olivia. I have no idea what Marsallas's plans are for the villa. But I promise you, I will try my utmost to find out and let you, and the other, slaves know."

"Thank you, Mistress. You...you have always been so kind to me."

Justina never said anything more, and when Olivia had finished styling her hair the young girl bowed and left the room. For a long time Justina sat at the table, her mind racing, before she got up and walked over to the window. She hadn't said anything to Olivia earlier, but she had been thinking a lot about what would happen to her tire-woman. She had some money, not a lot, but she planned to ask Marsallas if he would be willing to sell Olivia to her. She couldn't bear the thought of the young girl being sold to someone else.

Pain lanced through her, and she wrapped her arms around her middle as she remembered the time five years ago when Olivia had first arrived at the villa. She had only been thirteen, bought from the slave markets to serve Justina's every need.

But what Olivia didn't know at the time was that *she* had been a replacement for Justina's first tire-woman, Vibia.

Justina's heart lurched as she thought of the young girl. Vibia had only been fifteen, a year younger than Justina had been. But unknown to Justina at the time, as well as catering for her every needs, Vibia had been ordered to report everything that Justina did to Quintus.

She was, in effect, Quintus's spy...

So when Justina took it upon herself to escape from the villa one night, six months after she had been given to Quintus, she hadn't realised what the consequences of her actions would be.

The attempt to escape had been a futile one in the end. She'd had no plan, no strategy as to *how* she was to do it. Desperation had driven her to it. Being confined to the villa had driven her insane, so one night she had gone down to the pier and she'd just jumped into the water, intending to swim to the shore and run away. Her plan had been to get to Rome somehow, to find Marsallas, explain everything and beg his forgiveness.

But she'd never even reached the shore. She'd been seen by one of the slaves, who'd told Quintus, and a boat had been launched to fetch her. It had been Diogenes who had lifted her out of the water, as though she was some sort of exotic fish that he had landed, and who had taken her back to the villa, where Quintus was waiting for her.

She would never forget the moment she saw Quintus standing on the wooden decking of the pier waiting for the boat to dock. He had hold of Vibia by her hair in one of his hands, and a long thin whip, which he'd often used on the slaves, in the other. And when she had been unceremoniously dumped out of the boat to lie in a sodden heap on the wooden planks, *and* he was sure he had her full attention, only then had he thrown the poor girl down onto the floor and started to whip her. It was then that Justina realised to her horror that Vibia was being punished for allowing her to escape.

He'd given her twenty lashes; lashes that had cut through her clothing, causing her to bleed, and to this day she remembered the agonised screams of the poor girl as she lay crouched on the wood, her hands covering her head as she tried to protect herself.

But it was only when he'd finished whipping her that Justina found out what Quintus was *truly* capable of.

"Get her out of my sight," he'd ordered to one of the male slaves who stood silently next to him. "I never want to see her again. Take her to the local brothel and sell her,"

"No, Quintus, I beg you," Justina had pleaded, and on her hands and knees she had crawled over to him and pulled at the hem of his toga, "Let her stay, I beg you. I...I promise you that I will never try to leave here again."

But it had all been for nothing, and she'd watched in horror as Vibia was dragged away, kicking and screaming. It was the last time she ever saw her...

And as she watched Vibia being taken away, she had been was unprepared for the sting of the whip that lashed across her back when Quintus turned his fury onto her. Pain tore through her as she felt the sting of the lash slice across her skin. Over and over he whipped her, and like Vibia she tried to shield herself from the blows by wrapping her hands over her head.

Eventually, he stopped, and Justina was vaguely aware that he'd only stopped because of the intervention of Diogenes, who had stepped forward and grabbed his arm.

"Enough, Master." The two words were enough to jolt Quintus out of his blind rage, and he'd thrown the whip down next to her and stormed off back to the villa.

For several long minutes Justina lay on the floor, curled up in a tight ball of misery, before she felt herself lifted, unable to stop the exclamation of pain that tore through her.

"I am sorry, Mistress, but we must get your wounds tended to," Diogenes said, cradling her in his massive arms, "If we don't, they could fester and you could die," and with her whole body screaming in pain she was carried back to the villa.

The only good thing that came out of the whole sordid mess was that she came to know Lydia, who had been brought to the villa to tend her wounds, and who was to become a firm friend to her over the following years…

* * *

Justina took a deep breath, wiped her suddenly sweaty hands down her silk gown, before she knocked on the door to the *tablinum*, and without waiting for an invitation opened it and stepped inside.

She saw Marsallas leaning over a pile of papers and ledgers, a frown of concentration on his face, totally unaware of her presence. His dark hair appeared tousled, as if he had recently raked his fingers through it, and she had the urge to go over to him and brush it back to normality. But despite his dishevelment, he still looked totally in control. This was a man who knew his place in society. For a few uninterrupted moments she studied him, taking in his power, his strength as he sat at the desk. He was dressed in a blue tunic, the colour, she knew, would complement his eyes perfectly, and her eyes dropped down, taking in the finely honed muscles of his legs, down to his sandaled feet. Then unbidden her eyes travelled upwards, past the muscled forearms, the corded neck, and back to his face. He looked tired she thought—

"Did you know about these debts?"

The words were bitten out, interrupting her thoughts. She blushed in mortification as she realised that he had once again caught her staring at him. Not wanting to inflame what was already a difficult situation, Justina walked over to where he sat staring up at her with an inscrutable expression on his face. Firming her chin she said with quiet dignity, "Yes."

"And did it not occur to you to tell me about them?"

"I would have told you of course – but you were not here," she explained with calm logic before continuing, "I was about to send a messenger to Rome to tell you."

She heard Marsallas grunt, as if, reluctantly he accepted her explanation. Then pressing her advantage she said quietly, "I didn't even know you had returned to the villa until…last night.

"How long have you known about all of this?"

Justina shrugged slightly, "Since the morning of Quintus's death, when the creditors started to arrive at the villa." She hesitated for a moment before asking, "Could you contest the will? I'm sure Quintus never meant—"

"What would be the use of that, Justina?" He said harshly, "Quintus wasn't mad was he? Just ill."

Her shoulders slumped. He was right. There had been nothing to say Quintus had lost his mind. He had been the same as always. Cold and cruel, right up till the day of his death.

"You can go now," he said, interrupting her thoughts.

For a moment she hesitated, and Marsallas raised his eyebrows in silent command for her to continue. Justina lifted her chin slightly, "I…I would like to know what you intend to do with the slaves? Some of them have come to me with their concerns. I…I have a tire-woman, a young girl called Olivia."

Marsallas's eyebrows rose even higher, obviously surprised by her question. Shrugging slightly, he said, "I haven't thought of them yet. I'm still trying to sort out the mess my uncle has left me, but I haven't found anything here that helps me, though," he said with disgust, as he lifted a thick sheaf of papers from the desk.

"I looked yesterday as well. I never found anything then either."

"So you *have* been snooping around! Perhaps you did know what was going on after all!"

Justina stiffened at his barbed comment before retorting, "I wasn't *snooping*, as you so crudely put it. I was merely trying to find out exactly how much debt Quintus was in. *And* I told you the truth, I knew nothing of the debts until the day he died. Your uncle's creditors have been hounding me ever since he died. They think—" She stopped speaking abruptly.

"...that as his mistress you could pay them." Marsallas finished off, his mouth twisting in derision.

Justina chewed her bottom lip, "Yes."

The tension in the room was palpable, and eventually Marsallas spoke, "In answer to your earlier question I haven't thought of the slaves. How many of them are there?"

"Not many. Ten at the most. Quintus had been reducing their numbers over the past few years. I suspect it was to reduce his overheads, considering the debts we now know about."

Marsallas grunted again, running a hand through his rumpled hair before murmuring, "I think you are right. It would seem to make logical sense." For a long moment he said nothing, then he shrugged, "You can keep your tire-woman for now. As the former lover of such a prominent man as Quintus, you are expected to maintain a certain position here in Herculaneum. I will think about what to do with the other slaves once I have sorted this mess out."

Justina stiffened at the barbed insult, but she deliberately bit back a retort. Losing her temper right now would be stupid. She didn't want to antagonise him to the extent that he rescinded his offer of letting Olivia stay. So instead, she bit her tongue, and changed the subject. "I'm not sure if you know, but Secundus, Quintus's overseer, left yesterday morning." *Thank the gods...*

A wry smile flitted across his face. "Yes, I had heard. But I don't think it will be any great loss will it?"

Justina smiled back at him, before she shook her head, "No. No loss at all." Then she hesitated momentarily, before saying, "And I...I don't know if you are aware, but Diogenes has been given his freedom—"

"Diogenes!" At her words Marsallas stiffened, his face suffusing with anger, at the mention of the former slave's name.

Justina tried to appeal to him, "I know you hate him, Marsallas, but he was only carrying out Quintus's orders." She felt a pang of sympathy as she saw a myriad expressions cross his face. Then she firmed her resolve and continued, "You, of all people, should know what Quintus was like. If his orders weren't carried out, then he would punish the slaves without any mercy. And…and not just the slaves either," she added as an afterthought.

"What do you mean '*and not just the slaves either*'?" He asked, frowning up at her.

Justina shrugged, "He was a cruel man, that is all."

"You're lying, Justina. I'm in no mood for games, now I'll ask you again, what do you mean?"

Justina hesitated, cursing her wayward tongue. But realising she had no choice, she expanded, "He punished me as well."

"What for? How?"

Justina looked away from the intensity of his gaze, taking an inordinate amount of interest in picking an imaginary piece of thread off her silk gown. Then she answered slowly, "He sold my tire-servant – a girl called Vibia. To…to the brothel in town. She was only sixteen years old."

"What did you do to warrant such punishment?" The words were spoken quietly, as if he sensed her fragility in talking about what had happened.

She finally lifted her head and looked him squarely in the face, "I ran away."

"Why?" he asked, his voice was like silk, commanding an answer from her as he leant back in his chair and watched her.

For a heartbeat she considered telling him everything. But she felt too raw, too vulnerable to reveal her innermost longings, the hopes she'd had back then. So instead she gave him a watered-down version of the truth, "I…I was going mad. Your uncle forbade me to leave the villa, and I had nothing to do, day after endless day. One day I just couldn't take any more, so I waited until it was dark, and left."

"Obviously you were caught." The words were said drolly, and Justina blushed.

"Yes," she said, biting her bottom lip, "I hadn't got very far when Diogenes caught me."

68

She heard Marsallas grunt, saw a faraway look enter his eyes, as if he too remembered what it was like to be a prisoner here in the villa, before she carried on, "And to punish me for running away, Quintus took his revenge out on Vibia. She was, apparently, supposed to watch my every move, no matter what time of the day it was."

Marsallas said nothing when she stopped speaking, and thinking he had nothing more to say to her she composed herself and said in a soft, measured tone. "If I may, I would beg your leave to remain here in the villa for a few more days before I leave." And with that, she turned and walked towards the door.

"Wait!" Marsallas shouted, at her retreating back, "Leave? Who said anything about you leaving?"

Justina turned back to face him, "I…I can't stay here. This… this is your villa now," she stammered, when she saw confusion shadow his eyes.

Marsallas jerked his head slightly, his lips thinning, "Not for long, I imagine," he drawled, "I will need to sell it to pay my uncle's debt. Stay as long as you like. I'm not that heartless as to throw you out on the streets." Then as an afterthought he asked, "Where will you go, anyway, if you were to leave here?"

"I…I have friends. Lydia, your uncle's healer, and her husband Marcus have offered me a place to stay. But I haven't decided yet." She lifted a shoulder in a gesture of nonchalance, "I have some money of my own—"

Pushing back his chair, he advanced towards her, his eyes intent. "Where did you get the money from?" he barked, "I know my uncle never left you any in his will."

Justina hesitated in telling him, but then annoyed by the domineering tone of his voice, she snapped, "I earnt it by—"

"On your back no doubt!"

Justina gasped, and her neck jerked back in anger, her hand lifting to strike him, but as quick as a snake Marsallas grabbed it, roughly pulling her forward so she fell hard against his solid torso. His arms came around her, holding her prisoner, before his face swooped down and his mouth captured hers.

The kiss was a punishment, designed to humble and humiliate her, and Justina groaned in mortification as his lips ground down on hers, demanding her surrender. She tried to twist away, but her strength was no match for his, and she heard him chuckle deep in his throat, the sound resonating deep in his chest.

For endless moments the kiss went on, until, subtly it changed and Justina felt his tongue probe gently, demanding, and eventually gaining access to the softness within.

She moaned in longing as his arms slackened, allowing hers to creep upwards, until her fingers came to where the hair grew at the nape of his neck. Hesitantly, she ran her fingers through the silky softness, glorying in the texture, as the kiss deepened in intensity.

Like someone lost in the desert, and desperate for water, she drank him in, the smell of him, the taste of him, the strength of him...

Justina didn't know how long the kiss lasted, but eventually her subconscious realised that Marsallas had stopped kissing her, and slowly she opened her dazed eyes, pulling away from him, to see him staring down at her with hooded eyes, a dark stain of colour riding high on his cheekbones.

He lifted his hand to ward her off, as if she were an evil spirit of some kind, then he wagged a finger at her and whispered, his face hard, his eyes fierce, "You are good, Justina. Very good. One of the best I've ever had. You have learned the whore's tricks well."

The insult made Justina recoil from him, before she bit out, her eyes flashing, "I am not a whore, Marsallas. You will do well to remember that."

Marsallas raised his eyebrows, "That's as maybe, but six years as my uncle's mistress you have learned to kiss well."

"I repeat. I am not a whore. Your uncle never took me." As soon as she had spoken the words, she saw disbelief cross his face, and unable to bear his scorn she turned away.

70

She heard Marsallas laugh behind her, the sound hollow and false. "Your story is worthy of any of the plays I've seen performed at a Roman playhouse!"

"It's the truth, I tell you," she hissed, turning back to face him once more, anger making her bristle and spit like a frightened kitten. "Your uncle never took me. Why don't you believe me?"

Marsallas stepped closer, his large hand tilting her chin up so she had no option but to look up into his hooded gaze. "Because my uncle came to Rome six months after I left this villa. He told me how he had taken you every night. Taught you all manner of things in his bed. He even told me you had become pregnant but had lost the child. So trust me, when I say there is *nothing* you can say that will convince me otherwise, Justina. So don't embarrass yourself any more by trying to protest your innocence. You kiss too well to be convincing!"

The silence in the room was deadly, and then as if things could not get any worse Marsallas said, "And as we are talking about 'truth' Justina. Just what *is* the truth? You pledged your love to me on your sixteenth birthday as we lay on the sand over there," he said gesturing with his hand to the nearby beach. "Do you remember *that?* We were to be together. I was even going to ask you to marry me. Then I found out later that evening that you were to be my uncle's mistress. So don't tell me what the "truth" is Justina. I saw the truth all those years ago."

She looked away, unsure how to answer him. Would he believe her if she told him the truth, told him everything? She lifted her eyes to his. "I had no choice, Marsallas—"

"There was always a choice, Justina," he interrupted, his voice bitter. "I *gave* you that choice, remember?"

Justina's stomach knotted in fear when she realised what he was referring to, but before she could say anything, he went in for the kill, his fingers tightening fractionally on her chin before he bit out, "I gave you that choice when I came to your father's bakery later that night and *begged* you to come away with me. But you just stood there, didn't you? You just stood there and told me that Quintus had the money to take you away from a life of drudgery, to provide you with everything you wanted." His lips twisted in disgust, as he glared at her, "Didn't you?"

She swallowed hard, "Yes. Yes I...I did, but—"

"Enough!" His eyes darkened in rage, cutting off her faltering words. "I once told you to rot in Hades, Justina. Well I hope you did, because I followed you there myself, and I've been there every day since."

And before she could say anything in her defence, he turned and left the study, leaving her standing there, her eyes haunted as she watched his tall, broad-shouldered figure stride out of the room.

Once he had gone Justina slumped to the floor in anguish. "But I had no choice," she whispered to herself. "No choice at all."

Then she moaned in despair. Was it always going to be like this between them? The past coming between them, destroying them, destroying everything? Never to be given the chance to heal, like some open, festering wound?

The truth was that she still loved him. As much – perhaps even more – than she had when she was sixteen. Her love for him hadn't died. It was as if it had lain dormant, curled up inside her heart these past six years, only to awaken once more on that fateful day when she had gone to his quarters at the Circus Maximus.

Yes, she still loved him. Still longed for him – even though he had – and still did – treat her abominably. And that was the point? What useful purpose did it serve if she built up enough courage to tell him the truth about what had happened in their past *and* confess that she still loved him?

He was so bitter, so resentful of her at the moment, that it would be emotional suicide to declare her love for him right now.

And he wouldn't believe her anyway. Quintus had seen to that! By going to Rome he'd sowed the seeds of hate. Planted them so deep that they were incapable of being dislodged.

She knew why he'd done it, of course. He'd gone to Rome

immediately after she had tried to run away. At the time she had known nothing of his trip as she had been seriously ill: a fever caused by the festering wounds on her back after Quintus had whipped her.

Justina closed her eyes as a feeling of restlessness swept over her. She needed to do something physical to get rid of the tension that was pulsing through her. Standing up, she quickly made her way out of the villa and headed towards the stable blocks, passing through the magnificent garden laid out to evoke the idyllic land-scape of Elysium, the Roman paradise.

When she reached the last of the blocks she opened a door and let herself in. She was momentarily taken aback when she saw Diogenes hard at work. He looked up at her, his body covered in sweat as he stoked the giant furnace.

"I didn't expect you here today. I thought you would have left."

Diogenes said nothing, but he did stand up straight, a frown of confusion on his face. Justina shrugged her shoulders slightly, "Your freedom," she elaborated, "I thought you might have left already, that is all."

Diogenes came forward, and then, much to Justina's surprise, he fell to his knees in front of her, "What—?"

"I want to ask your forgiveness, Mistress. I have wronged you," Diogenes said, interrupting her.

"I…I don't understand Diogenes?" She stuttered, taken aback by his words.

"All these years, I have had to obey the Master," Diogenes said slowly, his voice deep with the intensity of his feelings, "Do things that I didn't want to do. Spy on you, follow you, watch your every move, and then tell *him* everything."

Justina stood open-mouthed, amazed at what she was hearing, and amazed that he had spoken for so long!

"And if I didn't do what he asked, he would punish us all – you, and the other slaves."

"Oh Diogenes, I know that!" Justina implored, suddenly

understanding. "I know you had no choice but to do as he ordered."

Diogenes nodded, and then stood up. "I would like to serve you if I may, Mistress. I want to repay my debt to you."

"But Diogenes there is no need. I understand, truly, I do. You have the opportunity to leave this place, to make a new life for yourself."

"Yes I know, but I want to stay here. Help you with the furnace, with the sculptures."

Justina lifted her hands up in frustration, "But this villa belongs to Marsallas now. I doubt very much if he wants me here. I'm only staying for a few more days until I find somewhere else to live. And if I can't find somewhere, then Lydia has offered for me to go and live with her, and her, family…"

Her words trailed off as she saw a faraway look come over the slave's face. Relenting slightly, she said, "But I may very well need a bodyguard in the future, so if you wish to come with me then I would be most grateful, Diogenes." Seeing the relief on his face Justina smiled, before nodding to the furnace, "Now shall we get to work?"

Diogenes grinned, and for the next few hours they both worked together in a companionable silence.

CHAPTER SEVEN

Justina adjusted the fine silk scarf that she was using to cover her head. The heat from the afternoon sun was stifling as she walked down the near-deserted streets of Herculaneum. But the heat didn't bother her in the slightest, and she glanced across at Olivia, and smiled. The young girl smiled back, and then they both giggled like two young girls caught up in the excitement of their first unaccompanied trip into the town.

Ever since Secundus had left the villa, there had been a more relaxed atmosphere around the place, as if everyone could suddenly breathe more easily now he had gone. Since Quintus had fallen ill, the overseer had assumed total control, and he had done it without any compassion, ruling the villa with an iron will, enforcing his, and Quintus's orders, with a heavy hand.

But now he had gone, slinking away in the dead of night like a rat, and Justina couldn't quite believe that after all these years, she *finally* had the freedom to wander down the streets of her own free will! It was a heady experience that was only tainted when she came to what had once been her father's bakery. It was now a silversmith, and as she peered through the wooden shutters into the dimness within, she saw no evidence at all that it had once been a thriving bakery that she, and her father, had toiled away in day after day.

Justina sighed. It was all such a waste. Her father had been the best baker in the whole of the Bay of Naples. People had come for miles around to buy his bread, and both of them had worked hard to maintain their reputation.

But it had all gone wrong, of course. Her father's gambling addiction had been their downfall. The gambling, which she had been aware of ever since she was a small child, had spiralled out of control, and unbeknown to her, she hadn't realised that he had been borrowing money to finance it. Money, she found out to her cost that had come from Quintus. And when he couldn't repay his debts, her father had given her to Quintus in exchange for them.

Now, as she stared sightlessly through the window, her mind recalled how it used to be when it was just the two of them working side by side in the shop. She couldn't help the sigh of regret that escaped, oh, there was no denying that it had been hard work, but it had been rewarding work nonetheless. She smiled sadly when she remembered her father joking that the heat from the oven was so intense that he was convinced that Hades was nothing compared to the heat in his bakery on a hot summer's day.

And, as if it was only yesterday, she remembered how the shop had been laid out. Twenty-five bronze baking pans used to hang from the walls next to the oval oven, in perpetual readiness for the next batch of baking. It had been her job to clean the pans, as well as the shop itself, and she had been immensely proud of keeping everything clean and orderly.

At the back of the shop, in the courtyard, there were two blind-folded asses, harnessed to two huge round stone mills, and they had walked continuously in a circle, grinding the grain needed for the bread. It had been Justina's job to look after them, and she had treated them well, her father often complaining that they were too fat, and that she fed them too much!

To the left of the oven, there had been the dough room, where her father had worked every morning, rising before dawn to prepare the traditional eight sectioned loaves that his customers had demanded. Later in the morning, Justina used to come down from their small apartment to the rear of the bakery and help her father once the first loaves had been taken out of the oven and the shop had opened.

"Do you wish to buy something from the silversmith, Mistress?"

Olivia's words jolted her out of the past and back to the present, and she couldn't help the sigh that escaped. For a moment she envied the simple life she used to have. Then she shook her head and turned to where Olivia was looking up at her, a small frown on her face, "No. Nothing from the silversmith, I was just reminiscing, that's all," then she smiled, "Come, we shall return to the villa now. It is far too hot for us to stay out in this heat."

* * *

"Did you have a nice walk?"

Justina raised an eyebrow at the words, spoken drolly by Marsallas, who she saw, with a hint of annoyance, was lounging against the main gate watching her as she walked towards him. His arms were crossed over each other, and her traitorous heart and stomach clenched with longing at the handsome profile he made. His eyes though, she noted, were hooded, revealing nothing about what he was thinking.

Before she answered him, she dismissed Olivia with a small nod, noting with wry amusement that the young girl edged around him warily. Once she had gone, she replied cordially, "Yes. Thank you." Then, with a hint of defiance in her voice she asked, "Is there a problem with me taking a walk? Did you want me for something?"

Marsallas grinned, as a wicked glint came into his eyes, "Now there's a leading question, wouldn't you say?"

Justina flushed in embarrassment, and dropped her gaze from him, totally ruffled by the almost boyish look on his face. It had been so long since she'd last heard amusement in his voice.

Thankfully he changed the subject and asked casually, "How is your father these days?"

Justina looked up at him quickly, as understanding dawned. He must have thought that she had gone to visit him. "He died four years ago," she said flatly.

Marsallas stiffened, his smile fading. "I didn't know. I'm sorry. What ailed him?"

Justina hesitated before answering, "I don't know. I only found out that he died two months after he was buried."

"Two months! But surely Quintus would have told you sooner? Permitted you to go to his funeral?"

Justina shrugged, "Quintus never told me anything, Marsallas. I thought *you* of all people would know how he was – how he treated everyone – so why would he change for me?" And with that she walked past him, her head held high and her back ramrod straight, leaving him to stare after her, a frown once again marring his handsome face.

* * *

"Where is your Mistress?" Marsallas asked later that afternoon as he walked into Justina's bedchamber only to find a young girl readying the room.

Startled, the girl looked up at him and stuttered, "She...she is in the stables, Master."

Marsallas nodded, and was just about to leave when a thought struck him. "You are Justina's tire-woman? Olivia?"

"Yes...yes, Master."

Marsallas nodded at the young girl, who was staring at him with a fascinated gaze on her expressive face, before he turned and left the room and headed out towards the stable blocks.

As he walked through the garden, he couldn't help but notice the sheer numbers of bronze statues that had been placed all along the whole length of the garden. There must have been in excess of twenty of them, and he wondered how on earth his uncle could have afforded them. They would have cost him a small fortune.

They were all magnificent, though, and whoever had sculpted them was very good. For a moment he stopped, his eyes drawn to a full-size replica of the Lance Bearer, the famous athlete. He knew the sculpture was a copy, as the original was by Polyclitus a Greek sculptor who had died over five hundred years ago. But nonetheless, this copy was superb! Whoever had done it had captured it perfectly, apart from the face, as that looked like—

Marsallas baulked at what he saw, when he realised that the face looked exactly like his! Blinking, in case he had suddenly gone mad, he leaned closer and looked at the sculpture in detail.

By the gods it was him! But how? Had his uncle had the sculpture commissioned to remind him of his lost nephew? It was possible of course – but highly unlikely. His uncle wouldn't have wanted a permanent reminder of the nephew who had disobeyed him from the first moment he had arrived at his villa at the age of five. A nephew he had only taken in because it was his "duty" to look after him after his brother and sister-in-law had been killed by bandits who had ambushed them as they journeyed along the Apian Way.

Marsallas shook his head in disbelief and carried on towards the stable blocks, only to find the first one empty, both of horses and people. The second stable block only had one horse in it – his. As Marsallas patted his horse, he murmured softly, "All alone, my friend? Where is everyone?" The horse just tossed his head. Marsallas took some apples that were kept in a small wicker basket nearby and fed his horse a treat. Once he had finished, he went into the next stable block but once again found that one empty too.

Where in Jupiter's name was Justina? Frowning, he walked back into the courtyard, and he was about to leave when he heard a noise coming from a small outbuilding that was set a short way back from the stables. With purposeful strides he headed for it, and without invitation swung open the door.

The first thing that hit him was the heat. It was as hot, and dark, as he imagined Hades would be. For a moment he let his eyes adjust to the dimness within, before he stepped inside. Then he came to an abrupt halt, as his disbelieving eyes took in what lay before him. For there, covered in a thick old woollen gown, was Justina, standing in some sort of sand pit. She had her back to him, totally unaware of his presence, as she waited for a sweat-soaked Diogenes to finish pouring molten metal into a clay cast that was standing upright in the sand pit.

Then reality hit him with the force of a hammer. *She* was the sculptor. All those bronzes in the garden had been made by her…

* * *

Justina wiped the sweat from her brow with a piece of woollen cloth, watching as Diogenes carefully poured the molten bronze into the cast. They both knew that this was the most delicate part of the operation, as one false move would render the cast worthless, especially if air managed to get in.

But with a practice borne out by over five years of experience, she saw that he had once again done a good job. She let out a sigh of relief that it had gone well, and looked up at Diogenes to thank him. But her words were never spoken, as she saw that he had stopped what he was doing and was staring at the door.

Justina had been concentrating so much on her work that she hadn't even noticed that someone else was in the room. She whirled around, felt her stomach drop when she saw Marsallas watching them, a dumbfounded expression on his face. She felt a small glow of satisfaction flare inside, that for once she had managed to ruffle his feathers *and* pierce his harsh demeanour.

Justina held onto that, and taking the opportunity it presented, she beckoned him over with her hand, calling out, "Come in, Marsallas, and see how I earn my living. As you can see, it is not on my back as you implied, but by sheer hard work!"

CHAPTER EIGHT

"So all of these have been made by you?" Marsallas asked later, as they walked through the garden.

"Yes." Justina nodded, "There is about a year's worth here."

"A year!" Marsallas exclaimed, "How long have you been sculpturing?"

"For over five years now. I started after—"

Marsallas frowned, "After what?"

For a few seconds an uncomfortable silence fell between them, but then Justina shrugged, "I started sculpturing after I ran away. Quintus thought it would be for the best. Something to occupy my mind."

Marsallas glanced quickly at her, noting that she looked ill at ease for some reason. There was obviously something amiss here, he thought. He was just about to ask her why when she said, "You could sell all these, you know," waving her hand to encompass all the bronze sculptures. "To…to help with the debts, I mean. I'm not sure how much they will fetch, but it will be something. Quintus used to sell the ones I made before, I don't know how much he got for them, but he must have made a profit because he let me carry on."

"Why didn't he sell all these remaining ones, if he could make money out of them?" He asked, nodding at the remaining bronzes.

"Once he became ill, he lost interest in everything. I offered to sell them for him, but he refused." Justina replied before she shrugged her shoulders gently, "I don't know why."

Marsallas said nothing, but inwardly he knew the answer. If he was right, then it was because Justina's sculptures would have fetched a good price, and his uncle wouldn't have wanted her to find out how much they had sold for. They must have made a good price, because Quintus wouldn't have let her carry on. His uncle *never* did anything unless it profited him somehow, and if he was right, he would probably find some bill of sale, hidden away somewhere detailing the amount they sold for. His uncle wouldn't have wanted his mistress to find out how much money her sculptures made, because *that* would have shifted the power from him to her. And as Marsallas knew to his cost, everything his uncle did had been done from a position of power.

Power over everything, and everyone.

For a few minutes they walked in a companionable silence, until he stopped next to the sculpture of the Lance Bearer he'd spotted earlier. "This is an excellent one. When did you do this?"

He saw Justina blush, before she answered hesitantly, "It was my first sculpture. I...I never sold it."

He glanced quickly her, but she was looking at the sculpture, a faraway look on her face. Softly, he said, "It looks like me, but when I was younger."

For several tense seconds he thought Justina wasn't going to say anything, but then he saw her nod, "Yes. It was based on you. I didn't have anyone else to use as a model at the time, so I worked from memory."

* * *

Justina glanced up at Marsallas from under her lashes, watching as he stared down at the sculpture with a frown on his face. For a moment she was tempted to say that she had kept the sculpture because it reminded her of him. That it had been her only link to him, her only memory of him. But she didn't. She wasn't prepared to drop the guard she'd built around her bruised and battered heart ever since he'd come back into her life.

"Why didn't my uncle sell it?" Marsallas asked, breaking into her thoughts. His gaze was penetrating, the blue of his eyes so intense she wanted to look away.

"I refused to let him sell it, because the proportions were not right. It was my first sculpture, my first experiment, so to speak, when I first started using bronze." Justina shrugged, striving for indifference, unable and unwilling to tell him the truth and the real reasons as to why she had kept it.

At her words, Marsallas's face hardened, before he nodded slowly. "Bronze maybe. But *I* remember you sculpturing me in sand. Hour after endless hour I posed for you, didn't I?"

Justina had no choice but to nod her assent, annoyed with herself for stirring up the past between them once again, and she braced herself for what he would say next. She didn't have long to wait.

"Ah yes. The folly of youth. Well-rest assured, Justina, I am no longer the gullible fool I once was."

* * *

Justina paced the floor of the bedroom, waiting for the appointed hour, a frown of worry on her face.

"Would you like me to dress you, Mistress?"

For a few seconds Justina said nothing, only half-aware of what Olivia was saying. Then she came out of her reverie, and focused on what the young girl was asking.

"What? Oh yes. Please. The cream silk will be fine." Justina said her voice faraway.

For the past few hours she had been in a state of flux, ever since she had received a message from Marsallas requesting that

83

she attend the evening meal. The message had taken her aback. After his terse words earlier, she couldn't think why he'd want to invite her to share the evening meal with him. Surely, she was the last person he'd want at his side?

Once Olivia had finished dressing her and tending her hair, she quelled the knot of fear that had pooled in the pit of her stomach and left her room, heading for the *triclinium*.

As she approached, she nodded to the slave who stood next to the door, taking a quick, calming breath as he opened the door for her to enter. She saw him instantly, reclining on one of the couches, looking totally at ease. He was wearing a tunic of dark-blue silk, the colour complementing his eyes, making them appear lighter, she noted absently. She watched mesmerised as he lifted his goblet of wine to his lips, the muscles of his arm bunching with the slight movement, and Justina felt her stomach knot, heat pooling there.

He was a superb specimen of manhood and a spasm of jealousy surged through her at the thought of him with other women. But she knew that she was being irrational. She had no claim over him whatsoever, and it would be pointless for her to ever dream that it could be so. But it still—

"Ah, Justina. Come in, take some wine."

Justina relaxed slightly when she heard the cordial tone of his voice. Stepping into the room, she took a couch directly across from him, preferring, for some reason to have a table between them.

If he noticed, he never said anything. Instead, he sat up and poured her a glass of wine from a gold decanter, before leaning forward to pass it over to her. She nearly dropped it when his fingers grazed hers, sending rivulets of pleasure through her. That, and the heady scent of his skin, was doing serious damage to her equilibrium, and striving for normalcy, she took the goblet, hoping he hadn't noticed her reaction to him as she lay down on the silk-covered couch.

"I have managed to sell the villa."

Her thickly lashed eyes widened. "So soon?"

84

Marsallas nodded, "Yes. I have done a deal with a prominent merchant in Pompeii. I got a good price, considerably more than I was expecting, actually. The sale of this villa and some of my own money will settle all my uncle's debts."

Justina bit the inside of her bottom lip. Marsallas sounded resigned to the fact that he'd had to bail out his uncle, but Justina simmered with anger at the way his uncle had treated him. Cheated him even, and unable to stop herself she blurted out, "But it isn't right that you should have to spend your money," she said heatedly, "Quintus only changed his will at the last minute, I'm sure of it. Cnaeus should have inherited everything, including Quintus's debts—."

"Who in the name of Hades is Cnaeus?" Marsallas demanded.

Justina realised that she had once again said too much, but having no choice she answered him, her voice soft, "He was Quintus's adopted son. He was to have inherited everything. It is my guess that Quintus only changed his will when he realised that he didn't have enough money to pay his debts, that…that they would probably surface when he died and—" She stopped short, unwilling to go on.

Marsallas frowned, "And?" he demanded

Justina looked up at him, her eyes full of sympathy, before she said quietly, "And I… I think he saw his debts as an opportunity to punish you – from beyond the grave."

Marsallas closed his eyes briefly, before he said bitterly, "Now why am I not surprised to hear *that*. My uncle ran true to form, even on his deathbed!"

"Why did your uncle hate you so?" The question popped out before Justina could stop herself.

She didn't think he was going to answer her, as the silence lengthened between them. Then, finally, he said, "Because I tried to kill him!"

Justina's mouth formed an "O" of surprise. "Really?"

Marsallas's mouth twisted in remembrance, his voice full of

hatred, "I was about ten years old when my aunt died. Up until then she'd had ten miscarriages and ten dead babies. I once heard her begging him not to have any more children. But he didn't listen, he *never* listened. She was his wife, he'd say. It was her *duty* to give him an heir."

Marsallas stopped abruptly, his face far away as he remembered the past. Then he carried on, "She fell pregnant again, but died in agony delivering another dead baby. Ten minutes after she died I took a dagger and tried to stab him. I didn't succeed, of course," Marsallas grunted softly at the memory, "And he beat me with his bare hands. I don't think I was able to walk for a whole month. But I didn't care. And the older I got, the more rebellious I became, refusing to obey his endless orders," he shrugged his shoulders, "Maybe it was because I wanted to do something more with my life, rather than have to follow in his footsteps. A life as a merchant selling Garum did not appeal!" He laughed bitterly, "So there you have it. I was a disobedient nephew, resentful about the way he treated my aunt, and resentful of him."

Justina said nothing, for there was nothing to say.

"Did you know you were one of many mistresses?"

Shocked Justina breathed, "No!"

"Umm, it's true. My aunt was his only wife. After she died the women came thick and fast, until I lost count, or cared, who came to his bed – until you!"

An ominous silence fell between them, and Justina felt compelled to say something, "Marsallas I—"

But Marsallas interrupted her saying softly, "I must admit, I expected to see children here, though. A fine healthy specimen such as yourself should have produced a child a year. So why are there no bastard children running riot around the place?"

Indignation flared through her. How dare he?! "I told you once before, Marsallas, that I never slept with your uncle. If you choose not to believe me, then that is your problem." And with that she stood up, unprepared to stay for one more minute in his company.

She may have no status in the villa any more, but that didn't mean he could keep insulting her at every turn.

"I'm sorry. Please sit. I will speak no more of it."

Justina hesitated. Should she stay? He hadn't said anything about believing her. That she hadn't slept with Quintus. *But* he had apologised. For a moment she wavered, undecided, but then several slaves entered the room carrying large platters filled with all manner of food, and she relented.

She sat down once again and ignored him, taking a selection of food off the platters. The small task gave her something to do, and it went some way towards breaking the tension in the room.

"I found out an interesting fact the other day. About your sculptures," Marsallas finally said, once they had eaten and the slaves had taken their leave.

"Really?" she said, keeping her voice cool, level, not prepared to let him bait her again.

He smiled slightly, "Yes, really. Apparently you are in great demand. Your sculptures are considered great works of art, both here in Herculaneum, and in Pompeii, *and* Quintus made a handsome profit out of them. As part of the sale of this villa I managed to persuade the new owner to buy all the bronzes left in the garden. Except the Lance Bearer. I thought I might keep that one."

"Oh…I…" Her words trailed off, as she couldn't think of a single thing to say in response to his last remark. A thousand questions burned in her brain, but she seemed incapable of voicing them. Instead she asked, "When will the sale go through?"

Marsallas shrugged, his mouth flattening, "A week, maybe two."

"I will be ready to leave by then."

Marsallas frowned. "Ah yes. Your departure," he said slowly, "I have been thinking about *that* a lot."

Justina shifted on her seat, unsure where he was going with this conversation.

"You said you will live with friends when you leave here. Correct?" Marsallas finally said.

Justina nodded, "Yes, with Lydia and her husband Marcus. I hope to stay with them until I have saved enough money to buy or rent my own studio."

"How much money would you need?"

"I don't know," Justina, said slowly, "Enough for a small house, with outside space for a furnace so I can carry on with my bronzes."

Marsallas nodded, crossing his arms over his chest and she watched transfixed as he smiled across at her. "Perhaps I can help. I have a proposition."

"Marsallas," Justina said hotly, "I told you I won't—"

"A business proposition, Justina," he interrupted.

Justina frowned, her eyes narrowing in suspicion, but she said nothing.

"The stables I ride for have been trying to get me to pose for a sculpture, which I understand they want to display at the Circus. I have resisted so far, but now maybe is the time for me to consider it."

Justina gasped at his words sank in. *The Circus Maximus! One of her sculptures to be displayed at one of Rome's great buildings! Was he serious? Or was it another of his taunts? If he was telling the truth then it would be an immense honour. The exposure would give her a chance to prove herself, to make something of her life—*

"You will be paid well." Marsallas said, interrupting her rapid thoughts. He named a sum that made her mouth fall open, "And I imagine it will be enough for you to buy a property, and to set up your business."

Justina said nothing, incapable of speech and Marsallas lifted a hand casually, "Think about it for a while. I don't need a decisions just yet, maybe—"

"No!" Justina exclaimed, finally finding her tongue, "I...I mean yes. Yes, I'll do it."

Marsallas nodded, his eyes hooded, before an unreadable emotion flickered across his face. "There are two conditions though."

Her features furrowed in confusion, to be immediately replaced by suspicion. She lifted her chin fractionally, "And they are?"

"One. You will come to Rome, or more precisely, to my villa to do the sculpture. I've no intention of *ever* returning to Herculaneum. And two..." He hesitated before continuing, "And two...I want you to be my lover. But only for one night."

Justina's face drained of all colour. *His lover? For one night? Had she heard him correctly?* One look at his hard indomitable face told her that she had, and her stomach clenched. She would be lying if she didn't admit to herself that his proposal both shocked and thrilled her.

She lifted her chin higher, "Why only one—" She couldn't go on, and hot colour suffused her whole body.

"Why one night?" Marsallas asked, finishing off her question. He rose from his couch and walked over to where she sat, tilting her chin up with his calloused fingers to stare deeply into the grey depths of her eyes. "We have unfinished business you and I. The day of your sixteenth birthday, do you remember it?"

Justina's eyes widened in remembrance.

"I see that you do," he said softly, "We would have made love on the beach if it had not been for your father finding us. I *want* that day back. I *want* what should have been mine before *you* betrayed me!"

At his words she couldn't stop the tears that sprang into her eyes, and she trembled with emotion. But if he felt it, he didn't relent, as his eyes were as hard as marble. She tried to pull away from his grip, but his fingers tightened on the softness of her jaw, holding her immobile, refusing to let her go, as he stared at her with such intensity that her whole body quivered.

"Am I to be your whore, Marsallas?"

Her words caused him to grit his teeth, and she saw the flush of colour that stained his sharp cheekbones.

Then he dealt his death blow. "Don't think for one minute that I want you for more than one night, Justina. You will give me your body, as payment for the turmoil you put me through six years ago." He leaned forward, his lips brushing against the softness of her neck. "You are the spoils of war, Justina. And I want to find out how sweet revenge can be."

CHAPTER NINE

Where was everyone? Justina wondered, looking around the empty compound, a frown of confusion on her face. She was sure Lydia, or another member of her family would be here, after all she had sent a message earlier to tell them that she was coming.

She was just about to leave when a door opened to one of the outdoor buildings and Justina saw with some relief Lydia emerge holding hands with her husband Marcus, followed by Caratacus, Lydia's father.

"Justina! I'm sorry we are late. Come in, come in," she said gesturing her over.

"I…I thought you might have gone somewhere, out for the day."

"No. No. We were praying," the older woman said, interrupting Justina's faltering words.

At Justina's confusion, Lydia smiled and came over to the young woman. Placing a hand on her arm she guided her back to the small building they had just exited.

As they walked inside, Justina's eyes adjusted to the dimness within, and she saw that the room was bare except for a small table that had been placed along a back wall. Above the table there was wooden crucifix.

"I don't know if you have heard of a religious group known as Christians?" Lydia asked quietly, watching the myriad expressions crossing Justina's face.

Justina frowned, "I think I have. I remember hearing something a long time ago about how the Emperor Nero had persecuted them, blamed them for starting the great fire of Rome. They worship a man called Jesus?"

Lydia nodded, "Yes, that's right. We do."

At her startled look, Lydia walked into the room and stood next to the crucifix. "We call Jesus our Lord, the one true God. We believe that he died for our sins. We worship him here with this cross."

At Justina's perplexed look, Lydia laughed softly. "I don't expect you to understand."

For a long moment Justina said nothing as she collected her thoughts. Then making up her mind, she said with a firm nod of her head, "I might not understand fully, Lydia. But one thing I *do* know is that, if worshipping your God makes you, and the rest of your family, the wonderful people that I have come to know and love, then that cannot be such a bad thing."

Lydia's shoulders slumped in relief, and she smiled, a radiant smile, "Thank you Justina for not judging me – us."

Justina turned from where she was looking at the crucifix hanging on the wall, and hugged the older woman. "I would *never* judge you Lydia, not after all the help you have given me these past years," she said, tears filling her eyes.

* * *

Later, as Justina sat with the rest of the Lydia's family enjoying a light supper, she thought with amazement at how extraordinary a life they'd all had. She had been told how they had fled Nero's persecution, and had ended up here in Herculaneum, where they had managed to settle and start a business and raise their family in relative peace with the help of their great friend Anna Faustina.

And how wonderful it must be for Lydia to be married to

such a man as Marcus! A man, who before he had met Lydia had been a Tribune in the army and most definitely not a Christian! But now, obviously after all these years, his love for Lydia had transcended everything.

In truth, she didn't really know Marcus that well. He was what Justina would call the strong, silent type. Always there in the background, strong, protective, but quite happy to let his wife, Lydia, do all the talking.

Now, as Justina looked at him from under her lashes, she hadn't realised how handsome he was. He must be over forty, she thought, but he appeared to be as strong and muscular as he must have been as a young man. The only outward change was his hair, now liberally speckled with grey. And Justina could quite easily see why Lydia had fallen in love with her handsome husband.

Just as she had with Marsallas.

Shocked, she blinked furiously, looking away from Marcus as her wayward thoughts overtook her.

Was she imagining herself with Marsallas, like Lydia and Marcus? She still loved him. As much as she did when she was sixteen. And that was the problem. She loved Marsallas, but he hated her. She just wished that one day, maybe, he could come to love her as much as she loved him. But she knew, deep in her heart, that it would be a huge mountain to climb – as huge as Vesuvius – the mountain that loomed over their town…

"I forgot to ask why you came to see us, Justina?" Lydia asked, interrupting her thoughts.

Blushing, Justina looked over to where Lydia sat, "Oh yes! I forgot. I wanted to tell you that I will be leaving soon. Marsallas had asked me to sculpt him. The team he rides for wants a bronze of him, his horses and his chariot to be displayed in the Circus Maximus—"

Justina stopped talking abruptly, realising that she was babbling. She saw Lydia frown, and her blush deepened further, before she said quietly, "It will potentially give me the opportunity to show the people of Rome my work. And…and from that one commission I hope others will follow."

"Are you sure, Justina," Lydia asked, "I don't want you to think for one moment that you can't stay here with us. I know the new owners are to move into the villa soon, but you don't have to do this if you don't want to."

Justina smiled, "It's got nothing to do with you, truly. It's…it's something I need to do for myself. I will be fine," she said a hint of resolve on her face and in her voice, "I am to be paid quite a lot of money, enough for me to set up my own workshop here in Herculaneum once I return."

Lydia sighed, and Justina saw her shoulders slump as she acknowledged defeat, "I can see that you are adamant about going, and to be honest with you I know *why* you would want to escape the villa, to have time to yourself, to be free for a short while, but—" she paused momentarily, "It is just that I worry about you. More so than my own daughter sometimes," she said with a slight laugh, "I just pray that you won't be hurt."

Her words trailed off and Justina blushed slightly as she took in Lydia's meaning. She was warning her against Marsallas. Justina could see that Lydia was worried that he would hurt her. Justifiably. There was no way of knowing what was going to happen on Marsallas's farm!

* * *

Five days later Justina left Herculaneum. Diogenes and Olivia sat next to her on the cart as they made their way out towards the city gates. But as they neared the gates Justina frowned, as a sudden thought came to her.

"Stop, Diogenes, please! I don't want to leave just yet. I need to do something before I go." And with that, she told him to turn around and head back into the town. A few minutes later the cart pulled up outside the single-storey building.

94

Diogenes turned to her and frowned, "Are you sure, Mistress?"

Justina smiled weakly, "Yes."

Diogenes looked at her for a long moment before he nodded. Then he leapt down off the cart and knocked loudly on the door in front of them, the noise magnified in the quietness of the empty street.

As they waited, Justina glanced at the crude drawings that were daubed on the walls and above the door of the building, and blushing she turned away, but then her eyes clashed with the eyes of a trader who happened to be passing by. At his knowing smile, she blushed even harder, and quickly turned her head away, taking an inordinate amount of interest in the back of Diogenes's bald head.

She couldn't blame the man for smiling at her. After all, he was probably wondering why a well-dressed young woman and her slaves were waiting outside the door of the local brothel waiting for it to be opened!

Then, thankfully, after what seemed an awfully long time, the door finally opened and a small fat man of indeterminate age appeared.

"Yes?" He barked at Diogenes, clearly annoyed at being woken up so early.

When Diogenes didn't answer him, merely stood aside, his arms crossed over his massive chest, Justina saw the man frown before he turned his attention to where she sat stiffly atop the wooden cart. At his raised eyebrows Justina finally found her voice, and stuttered, "I…I am looking for a girl…" But unable to think of what else to say, her words trailed off, and once again Justina blushed when she saw the amused smirk on the brothel-owner's face.

"Of course, my Lady." The man said bowing, well used to the proclivities of the rich. "I, Calpurnius Piso, the proud owner of this fine establishment have many girls. Girls that cater for all tastes, eh? Do you want her for yourself – or your slaves – or for all of you?"

Justina and Olivia both gasped in outrage at his words, and Justina saw Diogenes stiffen and move towards the man, anger emanating from his every pore.

Justina felt slightly better when she saw the brothel owner pale instantly, stepping backwards from the threat Diogenes posed.

"Diogenes, no!" Justina said quickly, afraid the former slave might hit him. "It is fine. I promise."

After a few tense moments, when Justina thought Diogenes might ignore her, she felt the breath she hadn't realised she was holding leave her when she saw Diogenes step back.

Relieved, Justina's eyes returned to the fat man, and she said quickly. "A slave girl named Vibia was sold to you nearly six years ago. Sold to you by Aulus Epidius Quintus. I…I want to know if she is still here."

"Vibia? Vibia?" The man repeated, frowning in concentration. Then his face turned angry as his memory recalled the girl. "By the gods yes! I remember her!" he snapped, wagging a finger at Justina in an unconscious gesture, before he carried on, his voice full of disgust, "I remember her all right. She only lasted a night!"

"She's dead?" Justina asked horrified, interrupting him, her face paling at the thought of the poor girl being killed.

Calpurnius laughed bitterly, "No, not dead. She ran away, or rather, she was stolen!"

Justina visibly slumped with relief when she heard his words, "Stolen? But who? Why?" She asked, unable to keep the excitement out of her voice.

Calpurnius placed his fat hands on his even fatter hips in a gesture of annoyance, "Well, if I knew *that*, I would have gotten her back, wouldn't I?" And with that he turned to re-enter the brothel.

"Wait, please! Just one more moment of your time. Please," she begged when she thought he was going to ignore her.

Huffing, the man turned around once more, his face full of frustration. Seeing the look of hope on Justina's face he relented somewhat, before sighing deeply, "All I remember was a small group of youths – sons of rich *patricians* by the look of them – coming in that night. They were in high spirits as I recall, and like all rich people they were very demanding. They wanted all of the young girls, and they paid me well for the privilege, if you know what I mean." For a moment Calpurnius was quiet, then his mouth twisted and he carried on with his story.

"Obviously, Vibia was ideal for their tastes," he said, a note of sarcasm in his voice, "One of them even declared that he had fallen in love with her at first sight!" Calpurnius's face darkened, before he added, "But then the next morning I realised she was gone. All I know was that the youths came from Misenum. I hired some men to find her of course – but nothing – it was as if she had disappeared into thin air. Poof! Gone!" He said clapping his hands to illustrate the fact that Vibia had vanished. "The only thing my men found out was that the youths were not from Misenum, they had arrived on a large ship a few days before, and for some reason decided to visit Herculaneum for their sport! Worse luck for me, though."

Then seeing that Justina hadn't anything else to ask him, he nodded at her and walked back into the brothel, slamming the door behind him.

The noise startled her out of her reverie, and she sat subdued next to Diogenes and Olivia as they finally made their way out of the city gates.

She wasn't sure whether she felt relieved, or not, that Vibia wasn't at the brothel.

She was relieved, obviously, that the young girl hadn't been forced into a life of prostitution, but concerned as well as to where she had been taken. She hoped that the youth that *had* taken her had fallen in love with her and that she now lived a life full of happiness.

Justina sighed, realising that in all honesty, and with a sense of finality, that she would probably never find out what really happened to Vibia…

CHAPTER TEN

The hairs on the back of Marsallas's neck prickled, and he narrowed his eyes. So she comes!

He watched the cart make its way over the hill and down the long winding road towards his farm. It had been nearly two weeks since he had thrown down his challenge, and he'd wondered if she would turn up. He thought she might change her mind, and if he were honest, he wouldn't have blamed her! But, she hadn't, and here she was, having taken him up on his proposition.

He squinted against the glare of the afternoon sun. He could make out three people in the cart. Justina, Olivia and Diogenes, if he was correct. He frowned, wondering why the slave still insisted on serving her when he had been given his freedom.

Stepping away from the window he walked back to his desk and sat down, carrying on with the paperwork he had been doing before he had been told of the imminent arrival of his visitors. Looking over to where Verus, his most loyal and trusted slave stood silently by the door, he finally said, "I would like you to show Justina around the farm, then show her the studio I've had converted for her—" He paused for a moment deep in thought. "And if she asks where I am, tell her you don't know."

The slave nodded before he bowed and left the *tablinum*, without a single flicker of emotion on his old lined face.

Once the slave had left, Marsallas stood up and walked back to the window, having had no intention of carrying on with his paperwork. He stood watching as Justina's cart came to a halt in the courtyard, watched as his slaves ran out of the villa to assist with their arrival. She enticed him beyond endurance. Was it madness to have let her come to his villa? Into his home. Now she would pervade it with her presence. Everywhere he went he would be convinced he could smell the scent of her perfume. Her own unique smell. What was he letting himself in for? *It's too late now* his brain mocked.

His face was grim as he watched the eclectic group finally gather all their belongings and go inside the villa. He had arranged for some light refreshments to be available on their arrival, but he had no intention of going to see Justina just yet.

He wanted to make her wait. Just like she had made him wait all these years.

* * *

Justina was leaning over a large box, a short while later, wondering what the packages inside contained, when a deep voice drawled behind her, "Open them. They won't bite!"

She jumped in fright, not having heard the door open. Swinging around, she saw Marsallas standing in the open doorway watching her. She stiffened slightly when she saw that he looked grim-faced as he watched her, and instantly Justina wondered what he thinking. *Was he already regretting her presence here?*

"I thought you were in Rome," she exclaimed, the blood pounding in her veins at the sight of him. He was so handsome, and her eyes were immediately drawn to his strong arms, his broad chest. She couldn't deny the physical attraction she felt for him. She'd wanted him six years ago and she still did.

"Now, why did you think that?" Marsallas finally said, cutting off her wicked thoughts.

Justina blushed, realising she had been caught out. Of course there was no reason why he *should* have met her when she had arrived but—

"Is everything to your liking?"

"Yes. Thank you," she said, her voice stiff, and trying to lighten the tension that once again hummed between them Justina shrugged, a resigned note in her voice, "You were sure that I would come then?" she said, gesturing to all the equipment he had provided.

Marsallas shrugged, walking down the small flight of steps towards her. "No, not really. There was a one-in-two chance of you turning up. I'm not much of a gambling man – but the odds were pretty good, wouldn't you say?"

Justina didn't answer his question, instead she asked one of her own, "All of this must have cost you a small fortune? You are most generous..."

Justina's words trailed off as he came to stand next to her, so very close to her that she had to resist the urge to step back. She could smell the enticing scent of him, a mixture of sandalwood and leather that caused her stomach to lurch in awareness of him. He was wearing a dark-brown tunic that moulded the breadth of his shoulders, shoulders she had the urge to run her hands over to see if they were as strong as she remembered. She imagined his mouth on hers, his lips tasting hers before they travelled down the length of her body. Wicked, delicious thoughts of his kissing every inch of her. Emotions long denied. His hands on her hips, his lips travelling to the softness of her stomach, kissing, nibbling the sensitive skin. Would he go lower? Would he taste her? She imagined he had no qualms about satisfying a woman in any way she wanted. And her breasts. By the power of Venus what would he do to her breasts? Lick them? Lave them? Suckle them until they peaked and demanded more. Would he bite them?

"The furnace will be here by next week. I have sent word for it to be delivered from Herculaneum, now that you have arrived."

100

Once again Marsallas's words interrupted her wicked thoughts, and she blushed bright red, amazed her wayward thoughts had got the best of her – again.

"T...Thank you. You are most kind."

Marsallas gave a short bark of laughter, "'Kind' is not a word I would use to describe myself, Justina," and then before she could say anything to that remark, he reached out his hand and took hold of hers, slowly pulling her towards him until they were within touching distance. Justina's eyes widened as she looked up into his face.

"You haven't forgotten our bargain have you?" His voice was soft, challenging.

Staring into his deep fathomless blue eyes, eyes that revealed nothing of what he was thinking, Justina whispered, "No. Of course I haven't."

Marsallas nodded, "Good. Because as I said, kindness is not one of my virtues," then he leaned forward and kissed her. Hard. The kiss was some sort of punishment, and Justina didn't know why. It was as if she were being punished for being here, for turning up at his farm.

She lifted her hands instinctively, placed them on his chest in a gesture of denial, fully intending to stop him by pushing him away. But she never got the opportunity, because a heartbeat later the kiss changed. The hardness of his lips melted away, replaced by soft nipping kisses that caused Justina's insides to melt. The hands that rested on his chest now crept upwards, over the corded muscles of his shoulders, until they met around the back of his neck.

She took delight in the moan that escaped him, pleasure spreading through her for managing to elicit such a response from him. He might give the outward appearance of not wanting her here, but his body said something entirely...

Eventually Marsallas pulled away, breaking the kiss with obvious reluctance if the colour high on his cheekbones was anything to go by. "We had better go back to the villa. You must be tired from your journey."

The words were uttered in a cool tone, and Justina stood back and looked at him. His eyes were hooded, revealing nothing of what he was thinking or feeling, as if he were waiting for something.

She looked away, unwilling for him to see how much he affected her.

"Time to go," he said softly, as if he knew *exactly* what she was thinking and feeling, and before she could react she felt Marsallas take her elbow and guide her out of the studio. Justina shivered at his touch once more, and if Marsallas felt her reaction to him, he never said anything...

"I understand Verus has shown you around the farm already," he said a few minutes later, as they walked across the courtyard.

"Yes. I didn't realise you had such a large farm, as well as a successful olive oil production business."

Marsallas laughed in amusement, "I'm not just some stupid charioteer you know."

"I...I never meant—"

"Justina. I jest." Marsallas said, a wry note of humour in his voice as he interrupted her stuttered apology.

For a few moments a companionable silence fell as they walked next to each other. Marsallas smiled to himself, secretly pleased that she now knew he wasn't just some mindless rider who chased chariots around an arena every day. He wanted her to see that he was a seriously rich man, who owned a string of farms and produced olive oil that was transported to all the four corners of the mighty Roman Empire!

He was proud of the fact that he had invested wisely, never squandering his money like some of the other charioteers did. He knew that his riding days wouldn't last forever, and early on in his career he had channelled all of his spare money into land. Once he had left his uncle's villa, he'd made for the Circus Maximus. He'd heard stories of men earning riches beyond their wildest dreams. If he could get in, make a name for himself, he was guaranteed to make money. And he'd wanted to do that with a passion that bordered on obsessive. Money was the way he would claw his way out of his miserable childhood. And he had succeeded. Way beyond his imagination. He was as rich – if not richer – than many of the powerful men who inhabited the Senate.

It was just as well that not everyone knew that, of course. He didn't aspire to a life of politics in the Forum, merely content with his lot here. His thoughts were broken when they entered the *atrium*, and he called one of his female slaves over and told her to take Justina to her room.

"I will see you later, at the evening meal, as I have work to do now." And with that he turned, leaving Justina alone once more.

* * *

He is a complicated man, she thought, as she stared at his retreating back. One minute cordial, the next abrupt and terse. She sighed, not understanding him in the slightest, and eventually she turned to where the young slave girl stood patiently waiting for her. With a small smile of acquiescence, she followed the slave, who took her off in the opposite direction to where Marsallas had gone.

* * *

"More wine, Justina?" Marsallas asked later, as they ate their meal in the *triclinium*.

Not wanting to break the cordial ambiance of what had been a very pleasant evening so far, Justina nodded, "Yes please. Another would be nice."

She watched as Marsallas went over to a cabinet and poured her a goblet of wine from a gold decanter. She had been slightly taken aback when she had noticed all the gold platters and goblets on display. It was obvious that Marsallas must be a very rich man, but he didn't seem to flaunt it as some did, and she admired him for that.

As he poured the wine, she could not help but watch him, her eyes drawn to his handsome profile. Tonight he wore a tunic of rich claret that complemented the tanned dark skin of his legs and arms; arms that were bare apart from a gold band that encircled his upper arm. The band was unusual, not the normal attire of Roman men, she was sure of that, and Justina wondered where he had got it from. But wherever it came from it suited him, made him appear virile, strong—

"So, when will you be able to start my sculpture?" Marsallas asked, coming to stand next to her before handing over the goblet of wine.

Justina blushed – a habit she seemed to be falling into a lot lately – at having once again been caught daydreaming! Slightly flustered, she answered, "I can start straight away with the drawings. I will need to draw you from all angles, and once that is done I can start making wax casts."

"Wax. Ah yes, I forgot to mention that I have asked a neighbouring farmer to provide you with all the wax you need. He has a lot of hives, so should be able to provide enough for your needs."

"Thank you." Justina said, pleased that he seemed to have thought of everything. "That is all I will need for now, until the time comes to make the clay casts..." Her voice trailed off, when she saw the intense brooding look on Marsallas's face as he watched her, suddenly becoming nervous.

For a few moments Marsallas said nothing, then he murmured, "Good."

Not sure what to do, Justina took a sip of her wine, looking away to stare at the flames that were burning brightly in a nearby bronze brazier.

"I didn't think you would come. What made you?"

The question caused a shiver of apprehension to run through her. He was so very, very dangerous. Like a lion stalking its prey he stood next to her. She had the urge to turn tail and run away.

104

But she stood her ground and shrugged slightly, "I don't know really. If I am honest, maybe it is the chance to show others my work. If your statue is to be displayed in the Circus, it will hopefully bring in a lot of work."

Marsallas nodded, "It will be. As I said before, I have resisted my stable's request to cast me in bronze up until now. Apparently, they want to display me above one of the gates leading into the arena," he said, before he murmured, "So it was for money, that you came here, in the end?"

His voice was soft, dangerous. "You should have taken a gamble on me six years ago, Justina. I had money, granted not as much as Quintus, but look at me now. *Now* I have a thousand times more than he ever did!"

Justina stepped back, her eyes flashing in anger. "It was never about money, Marsallas."

"Then what was it, Justina?" he asked, before his face twisted in disgust, "Don't tell me you preferred him. I won't believe it. I *can't* believe it. Your kisses, the way your body reacts to mine tells me otherwise."

Justina balled her fists, frustration and pain boiling over, "Is it to be like this all the time, Marsallas? You insulting me at every opportunity? If it is, then I'm leaving first thing tomorrow. I told you the truth. It isn't about money. It's about the chance to *finally* do something with my life."

For several moments Marsallas stared at her, saying nothing. Then he raked a hand through his hair in frustration, "I apologise," he finally said, his voice resigned, "It has been a long day and I need to return to Rome tomorrow. I plan to come back here as often as possible, but I have commitments at the Circus. I may only get back here once a week, if I am lucky. I hope that won't interfere with your work too much."

As an apology it wasn't much – but it was a start, and buoyed by it she said softly, "No…no that will be fine. T…thank you. And as you say, it has been a long day and I would like to retire."

He never said anything else, but his small nod of acquiescence was enough.

CHAPTER ELEVEN

"You are out of sorts this evening, Marsallas. Is there anything wrong?"

Marsallas turned to look at the beautiful young woman who spoke to him, noticing with wry amusement the frown of annoyance on her immaculately made-up face, and the way she just about held onto her anger as she drummed her fingers on the arm of the richly brocaded couch she was lying on.

And although the words had been said sweetly, he didn't for one moment believe that she meant them. Claudetta couldn't care less if there was anything wrong with him. The only reason she said them was because she was angry with him for being such poor company tonight. And being poor company, at one of her highly-sought-after gatherings was, in Claudetta's eyes, a major sin, and one that would not be tolerated at any cost! And now, as the last of the guests had just left, she finally got the chance to vent her frustration on him.

"Am I?" He replied at last, his tone laconic, as he bit back the smile that threatened, when he saw her face suffuse with colour, as her anger finally got the better of her.

Claudetta's lips thinned, her irritation coming to the fore, as she snapped, "Yes you are. *And* you know it."

Marsallas said nothing, but instead reached over to pick up his wine goblet where it sat on a low table. Raising the goblet to the woman in a silent salute, he took a deep swallow of the rich liquid.

Although he never said anything out loud, he acknowledged that in all honesty Claudetta was right. He *was* out of sorts, and had been ever since he'd left his villa – and Justina – and had returned to Rome. And as he mentally bowed to the truth, the wine he had just swallowed settled in the pit of his stomach, like some bitter potion, a punishment of sorts for the way he had treated her...

Justina – who at this very moment was currently residing at his villa fifty miles away, and who, from the first moment he had seen her when she had turned up at his quarters in the Circus, had dominated his every waking – and sleeping – thought. To such an extent that he felt he was going mad with it. The only thing he could think of to restore his sanity was to leave, which was why he'd left his villa last week at the crack of dawn, and had ridden at breakneck speed back to Rome.

Back to Rome. Back to some kind of normality, *that* had been his plan. Only his plan hadn't worked out quite how he had wanted it too. She made him lose the upper hand, and like a coward, he'd retreated to the relative sanctuary of the Circus. He needed to think long and carefully. He'd long since learned that it was foolish to base his decisions on immediate reactions. He'd always planned his strategies, right down to the last detail.

But she *still* dominated his thoughts, and he was still acting like some love-sick youth! And he didn't like it. Not one bit. But frustratingly, he couldn't seem to do anything about it.

What in the name of Hades was wrong with him? He should just forget about her. Just have sex, nothing more. Satisfying his hunger for her and be done with her. He'd done it with every other woman he'd slept with. Satisfy his physical urges and then move on with his life. Be like the other charioteers. *They* had women throwing themselves at them, day in, day out. But he'd been more particular. He'd taken a lover, on average, once a year. He used the distraction of endless racing, and his heavy work commitments on his farm, as a substitute for bedding women. The last had been Claudetta. A mistake. She had been far too controlling. And once he had wised up to her ways he'd finished their sexual relationship. She'd still wanted him, of course, and had insisted that they remain friends. Which was why he was here this evening…

Claudetta must have seen the myriad expressions that crossed his face, because she said in a deceptively soft voice, "Perhaps it has something to do with the visitors that arrived at your villa recently?"

Marsallas frowned in annoyance, but that didn't stop Claudetta, "I have been told that you are having a sculpture done – a bronze, *and* I understand it is being done by a woman – your dead uncle's mistress!"

Marsallas looked up at Claudetta, an incredulous expression on his face, seeing in an instant the hardness of her green eyes as they stared back at him defiantly.

She made a moue with her full, pouting mouth, the gesture designed to entice him with her beauty, "Now darling, don't look at me so. Of course I know what you are up to. You should know that as the daughter of a Senator – a very powerful Senator – I have access to *people*".

"'People!' Spies you mean." Marsallas shouted, anger evident in every line of his body as he stood up. "You have no right to set your spies on me, Claudetta. No right at all!"

Claudetta sat up slowly, annoyance etched on her immaculately made-up face, "I have every right Marsallas. As your lover—"

"Former lover, Claudetta. We haven't been lovers for months now." Marsallas growled, cutting off her words mid-flow.

"But…I still want you. You know that." Claudetta stuttered, for a moment caught off-guard, as she saw his thunderous expression. "I assumed—"

"You assume too much, Claudetta," Marsallas said, cutting off her words. Seeing the crestfallen expression on her face, Marsallas's anger dissipated a little, and he sighed in frustration, his voice less harsh as he continued, "I have always been honest with you, right from the very start of our relationship. We enjoyed each other's company – we had mutually enjoyable sex – and now it is over there are no hard feelings between us. Those were my terms and you took me, knowing what they would be."

He saw Claudetta turn away from him, anger in every line of her slim body as she absorbed his words. Raking a hand of annoyance through his dark hair as he watched her, Marsallas realised that there was nothing more he could say in his – or even her – defence. Sighing, he said quietly, "I'm sorry if you thought differently, but—"

"Leave me, Marsallas," Claudetta said, cutting off his words, dismissing him with a wave of her arm – as if he were nothing but one of her many slaves.

Marsallas stiffened, his mouth thinning in anger, annoyed with her once again for her supercilious attitude. He wisely held his tongue, having seen Claudetta's anger first hand on many occasions over the last year. Now was *not* the time to inflame it further!

Saying nothing more, he turned on his heel and made to leave the expensively furnished *triclinium* of the villa that belonged to her father. But just as he was about to open the door, Claudetta shouted, her voice full of bitterness, "I had thought that you, of all people Marsallas, would be too proud to take your uncle's leftovers, but obviously I was wrong."

Seething with anger, Marsallas resisted the urge to turn back and retaliate. Instead he flung open the door and stormed out. Obviously realising that she had lost her battle, Claudetta was determined to have the final word, "I hope your lack of commitment keeps you warm in bed at night, Marsallas," she shouted at his retreating back, "And I pity *any* woman who falls in love with you."

* * *

"*Uncle's leftovers.*"

Once again the words cut through him like a knife. The two words had been playing around in Marsallas's head for the past week ever since he had left the ugly scene at Claudetta's father's villa. Sighing, he shook his head, trying to dismiss the words but they refused to go, refused to be appeased.

He had been furious with her for spying on him. But then, knowing Claudetta as well as he did, he wasn't really that surprised. Nothing, and nobody, ever got in her way when she wanted something.

And she had wanted him. Right from the very first moment he had been introduced to her, at some gathering or another, she had practically chased him, refusing to leave his side all night and making it as plain as possible that she wanted him. At first he had been flattered, that the daughter of a powerful Senator had wanted him so much, and it had been inevitable that they had gone to bed on the first night of their acquaintance.

But as their relationship – if you could call it that – had continued, it had become more and more obvious to Marsallas that he was just some sort of pet project, her latest lover, her stud, who just happened to be the best in the Circus, and as such was to be paraded around her friends like some sort of trophy.

Marsallas has soon tired of it all, and he had stopped having sex with her. Claudetta had been furious. But because she still wanted him, she had been content to let him be a friend for now. Obviously, she had been biding her time, thinking that he would come around and be her lover again.

But that was never going to happen. He wanted Justina. But Claudetta's words had left a sour taste in his mouth. And he didn't know what to do about it—

"Ouch!" The pain that lanced through Marsallas's arm cut off his dark thoughts, "I said stitch, Fabius, *not* amputate!"

Fabius Rufus stopped his ministrations and looked up, smiling apologetically, "Sorry."

Marsallas grunted, saying nothing more as he looked down at

the deep wound. At Fabius's raised eyebrows Marsallas nodded, and the younger man carried on tending to the deep cut near his elbow, his brow creased in concentration as he sewed the flesh together.

Marsallas sat stiffly, sweat pouring off his brow as he endured the pain, waiting impatiently whilst Fabius tended to the wound.

"That is the best I can do I'm afraid." Fabius said a few minutes later, once he had finished bandaging the arm. "You should see one of the surgeons—"

"No surgeons, Fabius. They are nothing but glorified butchers," Marsallas interrupted.

"But the wound may turn septic."

"It will be fine. Thank you."

"Is there anything wrong, Marsallas?" The words were spoken quietly.

Marsallas stiffened, eyes narrowing as he turned to look at the younger man who was watching him, a frown of concern on his face.

"Wrong?" The words were spoken quietly, so quietly, that anyone who knew Marsallas would have known in an instant that he was angry. Very angry.

"I…I mean you no offence, Marsallas. But…but you have not been yourself recently. I know that your relationship with Claudetta has ended—"

Marsallas laughed harshly, interrupting Fabius's stumbling words, "By the gods the gossips – no make that Claudetta – have been hard at work."

Seeing the flush of embarrassment on Fabius's face, he took pity on the man. Sighing he continued, "I ended my relationship with Claudetta months ago. Believe me when I say that my ill humour has *nothing* to do with Claudetta."

"But you have been out of control recently."

Eyes narrowing in anger once more, Marsallas asked, his voice deadly, "Out of control? I don't think so Fabius Rufus. Perhaps you would like to expand on what you mean exactly?"

Fabius swallowed hard, but took the challenge thrown down by Marsallas. "You have been pushing yourself too hard, Marsallas. Ten races today. Ten yesterday, and every day before that, for that matter. It...it is too much – for you – and your horses." Fabius looked up to stare at his mentor, and friend, encouraged when there was no further retort. At Marsallas's silence he continued his voice earnest. "In all the years I have *known* you – *raced* with you – this is the first time I have ever had to *stitch* you."

Marsallas's anger evaporated, and he sighed, turning away to gaze sightlessly out of the window of his small quarters at the Circus Maximus. "Aye. Maybe you are right, Fabius," he said eventually, "I have been pushing myself too hard. But as I said earlier, it has *nothing* to do with Claudetta."

CHAPTER TWELVE

As Marsallas entered the room, he immediately spotted her, sitting on a small stool at the end of it. A large piece of papyrus paper was balanced on her lap, and she was sketching furiously, the charcoal stick in her right hand flying across the paper.

She was so caught up in her work that she was oblivious to him standing there. She'd been at his villa for nearly three weeks now, and this was the first time he had visited her since the night Claudetta had thrown her hateful words at him.

He watched as she lifted a hand to sweep a wayward lock of her dark hair away from her face, unaware that as she did so she smudged her cheek with charcoal. She looked tired, dark smudges under her eyes. But dishevelled or not, she was still beautiful, her thick black hair, loosely tied behind her with a thin strip of leather, the pale flawless skin, and the slender curvaceous body, all of which inflamed his senses like no woman had ever done. He'd never felt anything for the women he bedded. He knew he was known to be cold. Hard. But that was the way of it. He felt nothing beyond the physical. He was incapable of feeling anything more. He'd kept his emotions firmly in check. Always. His entire life since he'd left Herculaneum had never involved emotion. Never. Until now.

She was no longer the innocent girl he remembered; after all she had been with his uncle. She was now a full-grown woman, and he had vowed to himself, on those many nights he had lain tossing and turning with frustration when he had first run away from Herculaneum, that she would pay for all the pain and suffering he had gone through.

Claudetta's words still rang in his ears. He had, in turn, been outraged as well as deeply hurt by them. But then the truth always hurt didn't it? He'd tried to hold onto his simmering emotions for weeks now. But every day they had built up until he had been consumed by them. And now he wanted justice, revenge, call it what you like, for himself. She would pay the price for his lost innocence – and for the *bastard* he had become…

His eyes narrowed as he watched her. But how? That was the question that had plagued him for days now. What could he possibly do to Justina that would hurt *her* half as much as she had hurt *him*?

The answer had come to him two nights ago whilst in Rome, as he lain awake long into the night at his quarters at the Circus. His plan. His *revenge* for all the torment she had put him through these past years was simplicity in itself.

He would toy with her emotions, as she had his, until she didn't know if she was coming or going with madness – with desire for him. He would make her fall in love with him again. And then he would take her – the one night, as he had promised. But it would be *her* that would instigate their love-making. He could wait, he *would* wait. He had no choice – he was determined on this. And after they had made love? Well, he would walk out of her life without a backward glance, just as she had walked out of his…

* * *

It was only when she had finished her sketch that she became aware of a presence in the room, and belatedly looked up to see a man standing silently by the door. When she realised who it was, her face broke into a smile of welcome, "Marsallas! You have returned,

115

I was wondering when you would turn up."

Standing up, Justina walked over to where he stood, but stopped short when she saw the dark look on his face. Her stomach twisted. He looked in a foul mood, and she wondered why. Since his apology on the first day of her arrival she had hoped it would be a truce, of sorts, between them.

She watched as Marsallas walked down the small flight of steps towards her, until he was within touching distance. His gaze roamed around the room, taking in the many pieces of papyrus that were hanging on every available inch of the walls. All of them were of him – she had managed to draw him without him having to be present.

Then his eyes snapped back to hers, and still saying nothing he took the sketch she had been working on out of her hand.

"It is very good, as I knew it would be," he finally said, breaking the long silence between them. His blue eyes were intense as they stared down at her. "You've always had talent haven't you, Justina? I saw it when I was eighteen."

The words should have been a compliment, but they weren't, and her heart lurched. Could she ever get past the ice around his heart, and rediscover the warmth of the man she had once known? Would he give her a chance? Or had that part of him been lost forever, leaving nothing but the hard indomitable man who stood before her now?

"Is there something wrong, Marsallas?"

Marsallas smiled slightly, "Now what on earth could be wrong, Justina?"

He held his hand out in a silent command and Justina, without conscious thought, put her hand in his. The heat of his palm burned into hers as he tugged gently, pulling her towards him. They stood face to face, before Marsallas repeated, "There is nothing wrong, Justina, nothing at all."

He bent his head and she felt the heat of his breath on the side of her neck, his mouth tasting, nipping at the softness as if he were a starving man long denied sustenance.

The smell of him assaulted her senses, crisp tangy lemon combined with the smell of leather – totally him – and Justina's eyes fluttered shut at the gentleness of his caress. Suddenly, she was catapulted back to when they were young, to when they had loved each other unreservedly.

His lips moved upwards, towards the fullness of her mouth and she couldn't stop the involuntary gasp of pleasure that escaped when their lips finally touched. His hand moved up to her jawbone, squeezing slightly, communicating his silent demand, and she willingly opened her mouth, deepening the kiss, allowing, wanting, his tongue to enter. And when it did, it mated with hers in the parody of the love act, and Justina felt heat pool in the lower part of her belly at the sheer eroticism of it.

Then it was over. Reluctantly she opened her eyes, and looked up to see him staring down at her, his face once again a carefully concealed mask, his hooded gaze unfathomable.

The hand that had been cupping her jawbone lifted, and she felt his index finger trail upwards until it came to her cheek, and she felt him rub her sensitized skin.

"Charcoal," he explained.

His touch was as soft as silk, lulling her into a false sense of security—

"Are you ready to honour our bargain?"

His words acted as a splash of cold water, and Justina gasped, eyes widening in shock.

"Shall I take your body now – here – on the floor?" His mouth twisted in derision, "I am more than ready I can assure you."

His voice challenged her and Justina swallowed. He tempted her beyond reason. She wanted to do as he asked. Lie with him, strip him of his clothes. Run her hands over the width of his chest, to see if he was as strong as he looked. Oh yes. He was temptation in the flesh.

But the hardness she saw brought with it caution. It was obvious that he was angry and what to her had been a sweet kiss – an act of love – had meant nothing to him. She recoiled from him, shaking her head, wary of him once more. Her stomach roiled at the thought of spending time with him. How would she keep hold of her sanity? Her emotions? By the gods she had been a fool to have agreed to his proposition, she realised now.

But it was too late. She had given her word, and she would keep it. But it was obvious that their truce of the past few weeks was well and truly over.

What on earth had happened in Rome to make him so angry?

* * *

Justina sat on the wide windowsill in her bedroom, knees drawn up to her chest, her hands hugging them as she gazed out into the inky blackness beyond. Every now and again the moon peeped out from the clouds and she could make out shifting shapes, a horse in the paddock below her, some cattle lowing in a nearby field, one of the slaves walking to the stables to tend the many horses that Marsallas owned.

The hour was late and she was tired, bone tired, but still she could not sleep.

It had been over a week since the incident with Marsallas in her studio, one of the longest weeks of her life. Marsallas had left for Rome that very day, and she'd been left alone at the villa. She chewed her lip in frustration. What was the point of doing a sculpture of him if he wasn't here, wouldn't sit for her? She might as well leave.

Was that what he wanted? For her to leave, to concede defeat, to throw away all her dreams? Did he want her to fail?

"No," she breathed, "I won't let him win." Then a flash of inspiration hit her. *She had done all the preliminary drawings of him, and she roughly knew how the sculpture would turn out, so why not start the bronze without him?* If he didn't like it, then that was his problem – she couldn't wait around here forever, in the vain hope that he might, or might not, turn up. She had to make a life for herself. A future.

A pang of longing assailed her when she realised that her future would not include Marsallas. As much as she wished for it, wanted it, dreamed of it, she knew deep in her heart that it would never happen. His treatment of her last week was testimony to that.

A loud shout from the entrance to the villa interrupted her sombre thoughts, and she saw several slaves enter the courtyard holding torches aloft as they waited for someone. Moments later a horse and rider came into view. She could make out the rider's features in the flickering light, the harsh planes of his face cast into shadow, the unsmiling mouth, the firmness of his chin, the fluidity of his body as he dismounted his horse, before he handed the reins over to the waiting slave.

Marsallas had returned!

Justina's chin lifted in defiance. This time she was ready. This time she would fight her battles well…

* * *

The pale dawn arrived, bringing with it another day. She had lain in her bed for hours unable to sleep, her mind racing. Sighing, she rose from her bed and dressed in a lightweight gown. The weather had been unbearably hot and humid this past week and already the day promised to be the same.

Unwilling to summon Olivia, as it was still far too early, Justina brushed her long hair methodically, deep in thought. She was going to start on Marsallas's sculpture today, regardless of his return *and* whether he gave his permission or not! She needed to make some of the wax moulds, before she could start on the clay moulds which would eventually become the final bronzes. She had enough drawings to do that. What she *didn't* have was accurate drawings of his chariot. The only option left to her was to rely on her memory of him, and his *quadrigae,* the day she had come to the Circus to see him race. It wasn't ideal, but it would have to do. *She could do this! She would do this!* Her bronze would be the best, a focal point when entering the Circus.

She finally stopped brushing her hair, noticing that her hands were trembling with emotion. She had never felt such passion for one of her pieces before. She needed to, *had* to do this. Taking up a leather strip, she bunched up her hair and tied it back. She had a lot of work to do today, and for the next few weeks. She needed no distractions

What about Marsallas? Her brain mocked. Wasn't he a distraction now he was back? Her stomach clenched. What if Marsallas wanted her to honour their "bargain"? Was she prepared to do it? Did she want to do it?

She knew her capitulation was going be her punishment for breaking his heart all those years ago. Sighing, she stood up, annoyed with her wayward thoughts, and with a resolute tilt of her chin she left her bedchamber and headed towards the *triclinium* in search of some food.

But her resolve died the moment she entered the dining room. Marsallas was already there, eating some fruit from a platter that had been placed in front of him, looking totally fresh *and* totally at ease! He looked up, spearing her with his blue eyes. *Was that fire she could see lurking in them?* Then he smiled, beckoning her into the room with a wave of his hand, patting a couch to his left.

"Ah, Justina, come in. You are just in time to join me for breakfast."

Justina frowned at the light tone of his voice, totally at odds with how he had treated her last week. Tilting her head slightly, she came into the room, but pointedly ignored the couch next to him, instead taking one directly across from him, a low table separating them.

Her gesture, she noticed, was not lost on Marsallas, and she saw the wry smile flit across his mouth.

"Eat." He commanded softly, gesturing to the table laden with food, all the while watching her with hooded eyes.

Justina leaned forward and placed some bread and meat on a plate. She sat back and took a small bite, looking away from the intense look on his face, feeling soft pull of desire low in the pit of her stomach.

"How have you been getting on? Busy?" Marsallas asked a short while later, when the silence in the room threatened to overwhelm her.

Justina looked up from her plate and nodded, her tone slightly defensive, "Yes actually. I've done all the drawings I can, so I've decided to start the wax casts today."

Marsallas's eyebrows rose and he asked casually, "You have decided on a design then?"

Justina blushed, knowing that Marsallas could have added, *without my approval?* to his sentence. But refusing to be cowed by him, she leant back on her couch and affected a casual pose, meeting his challenge, "Yes. I've done all the preliminary drawings and saw no reason to wait." Then as her eyes locked with the blue of his, she added defiantly, "You can change anything that I have already done, if you wish."

Marsallas smiled fleetingly, "Put your claws away Justina, I'm sure it will be fine. After all, you are the expert, not me. I will be pleased to see what you have done in my absence." He paused, his eyes challenging hers, "I have neglected you recently, and rest assured, I intend to make up for that."

Then with a clap of his hands he stood up abruptly, "And as they say, there's no time like the present. So shall we?" he said, holding his hand out to her, the gesture giving her no choice but to place her small hand in his, as he pulled her gently up from the couch.

Justina didn't know whether he could feel the trembling of her body as he guided her out of the room, his other hand on the small of her back. If he did, he didn't say anything…

"You have done all this? Already?" Marsallas asked in amazement, once they were inside her studio.

Justina smiled, looking up at him. "I've not done as much as I would have liked, actually."

"Really? Well you could have fooled me." Marsallas said, as he picked up another drawing of himself. Remarkable drawings, totally lifelike, as if he were looking at his reflection in the stillness of a pond. "So what is outstanding?" he asked absently, still staring at the drawing.

For a moment Justina hesitated before answering, "I've had to draw your chariot and horses from memory. I don't think I've got the proportions quite right, but—"

"You've seen me at the Circus? When?" Marsallas demanded.

Justina blanched. Realising she had no choice but to answer, she shrugged her shoulders slightly, "I came to the Circus before my return to Herculaneum." She hesitated momentarily, "You were very good, by the way."

"I've had plenty of practice. Years of practice. To be honest I've had my fill of the place."

"But what will you do instead of racing? Isn't it your whole life?"

He shook his head, "I intend to spend more time here. I've got plans to expand my olive oil business. The Empire *always* has need for olive oil!" He broke off, deep in thought, "Funny really, I always hated the thought of being a merchant when I lived with Quintus. And now, here I am, considering being one myself!" Then he changed subject and asked, "So what happens next?"

Justina took one of the drawings she had done of Marsallas and explained, "From this drawing I will do a wax cast of your head and shoulders, mould it in clay and then I will cast it in bronze."

"Show me how you do it."

For a second Justina hesitated, unsure if Marsallas truly meant it, but seeing the earnest expression on his face she moved over to a table, where she took a large lump of wax and placed it on her turntable. Taking a knife she started to cut away at the wax swiping her knife through a nearby candle, heating the metal of the knife to make cutting though the lump of wax easier. Steadily she worked away, totally immersed in her work until the wax started to resemble a head.

"Once I have finished this, I will then start the process of the lost wax method."

"Lost wax? What do you mean by that?"

Justina smiled at the confused tone of his voice and looked over to where he sat, "Once I have finished the wax model I clean the wax to remove air bubbles and any imperfections. I then fill in any final details and depending on how complex the piece is, it can take hours, or days, to do. If my sculpture is going to be large, like this one will be, they are joined together and cleaned. Once the wax is ready, I dip it in clay, gradually building up layers as I go, to make a clay shell."

Marsallas, she could see, was frowning in concentration, and realising that he was still interested in what she was saying, she carried on, "Before the clay dries I need to make holes and vents, using wax rods and wires to make channels for the flow of the molten bronze. When the clay shell is finally finished, it goes into the furnace where the wax is melted out – the lost wax method. Once the wax has been burnt out clean, molten bronze is poured into the now hollow shell, and after the bronze has cooled the shell is broken open to reveal the new bronze."

"You make it all sound very simple," he said wryly, "But I'm sure it's not. How did you learn to do it?"

Justina shrugged, "Through trial and error. Quintus let me go to Pompeii to see another sculptor, who showed me the basics of what he did, but unfortunately for me he was very pompous and wouldn't let me cast a bronze of my own." Justina pulled a face, "He was of the opinion that that sculpturing was strictly men only, and that I was only there at his workshop on a whim. A rich *patrician,* obviously bored and in need of entertainment!

But thankfully, I was able to grasp the rudiments of what to do, and when I got back to the villa I was able to experiment.

123

For about three months I turned out bronze after bronze. At the beginning they were mostly rubbish, but I soon learned from my mistakes and got better. But, even now, after years of doing them, a bronze can turn out to be a disaster if you do not take the utmost care when you cast them. It is air, you see. If you let air get in, it will ruin the bronze, and weeks, months even, of hard work can be ruined."

Her voice quietened, "Working in bronze demands both an ability to let go and a trust that everything will come out all right in the end. And the final result is a piece of art that, hopefully, will last a lifetime, or even eternity."

Once Justina had finished speaking she carried on slicing away at the wax, and for a while a companionable silence fell in the room as she worked. Eventually, she finished what she needed to do for now, and lifted the wax mould to show Marsallas.

Marsallas moved over to the table where Justina sat and took the mould from her, turning it around in his hands, "It is very good, almost lifelike, as if I've suddenly grown another head," he said wryly.

Justina laughed, looking up at his bemused face.

Marsallas was smiling down at her, and she felt a glow of happiness inside her, reminding her of how they used to laugh and tease each other all those years ago on the beach in Herculaneum.

Caught up in the fun of the moment Justina went over to a shelf and took down a piece of wax. "Why don't you have a go?"

"Me?"

"Yes. Here, take this piece of wax and see what you can do," Justina said passing Marsallas the wax before he could change his mind.

Marsallas took it, a frown of concentration on his face. "What shall I make?"

"Whatever you like!" Justina said, holding back a small smile when she heard the hesitation in his voice.

For several minutes Marsallas worked on the wax, using her

knife to cut away at the wax, not forgetting to pass the knife through the candle to heat it, as he had seen her do, so as to cut away the wax more easily.

After about half an hour he sat back, a frown of annoyance on his face. "It's not working."

Justina looked over his shoulder to see a strange shape. Trying not to laugh, she asked seriously, "What is it supposed to be?"

"A dog."

"Umm."

"What's 'umm' supposed to mean?"

"Nothing. Just that it doesn't look like a dog, that's all." Seeing the brooding appearance on his face she took pity on him. "I think the knife got too hot. If you use the candle too much, it overheats the metal of the knife and the wax melts away too quickly. Trust me, it is a delicate balance between too hot and too cold that took me a long time to perfect."

Marsallas said nothing, but he did look up from the molten lump of wax in front of him to where Justina stood next to him.

"So I see." Then he smiled up at her, and Justina could not hold back the giggle she had been suppressing.

Growling in mock anger, Marsallas leaned forward and grabbed her hand, pulling her forward so she lost her balance and fell onto his lap. Instantly, she sobered when she saw the brooding look on his face, and without conscious thought she lifted her hand and traced it along his rugged jawbone, her eyes following the movements her hand made. It was as if her unspoken gesture was a signal of some sort, because he leaned forward and kissed her.

Justina gloried in the feel of his lips as they explored hers, tempting, teasing her with small nips of his teeth as he took what she offered. She didn't know how long the kiss lasted, but eventually he pulled away and Justina reluctantly opened her eyes.

"I want you, Justina."

The passion in his voice, and in his eyes, warmed her. "Yes," she whispered.

Her answer was enough to lay the ground rules between them, as if the barrier between what had happened in the past, and what would happen in the future, had finally been crossed.

"Soon?" He said, the one word both a statement and a question, and after a moment's hesitation, she nodded.

Then as if he'd had the answer he wanted, he changed the subject completely and said, "I can take you to Rome if you like, so you can do some proper drawings of my chariot and horses."

For a few moments she didn't take in what Marsallas was saying, so caught up in the pleasure his mouth had just given hers. Then his words sank in, and Justina's head jerked back in wonder, a wide smile on her face. She hadn't been expecting that. "Really?"

Marsallas nodded, "Yes, really. Be ready tomorrow morning at sunrise and I will take you. Bring Olivia and Diogenes with you. He can protect you if I'm not around."

CHAPTER THIRTEEN

To Justina, Rome was the most fascinating city on earth, and ever since they had arrived just over three hours ago she had been unable to contain her excitement.

Marsallas had secured accommodation for them in the same inn that she had previously used. But this time, as she watched the people coming and going from her bedroom window, she was able to take in so much more. This time she marvelled at the architecture and the sheer vibrancy of the city, fully appreciating all its multi-faceted layers. When she had been ordered here by Quintus all those weeks ago she had been too agitated, too nervous, to take in anything the city had to offer.

Which was why she was determined to make the most of it today. Marsallas had told her to take the rest of the day off, to get over the journey, telling her that he would see her at the Circus Maximus tomorrow morning, after breakfast, when she would be free to draw as much as she liked!

Turning from the window she looked over to where Olivia was putting away the few clothes Justina had bought. "Shall we go and explore?"

Justina laughed out loud when she heard Olivia's squeal of delight, and together they went in search of Diogenes.

As the trio walked out of the inn and into the Forum, they

were all instantly consumed by the hustle and bustle around them. The Forum was part market place, part law courts, part religious district and part political arena, as well as the place to get the latest gossip. And as Justina, Olivia and Diogenes walked under the three covered walkways that housed the many shops and offices, they watched in astonishment as the people poured into the Forum, which seemed to be reaching a crescendo of activity at what was the Roman fifth hour.

Plebeians, patricians, Senators rushed around making their way to the basilica or to the many shrines that stood either in, or around, the main square. The Shrine of Venus Cloacina, the House of the Vestal Virgins and the Temple of Caesar all seemed to be attracting many sorts of people. And as there were no vehicles allowed in the Forum from sunrise to the tenth hour, wealthy women were carried in litters by their slaves as they went shopping. Senators, marked out by their broad purple stripe-edged togas, walked down from their wealthy villas on the Palatine Hill followed, inevitably, by their group of clients.

As well as home to the rich, the Forum was also populated by quacks, soothsayers and charlatans, who seemed to dog Justina's every step, begging her to buy this or that. But even the constant pestering wasn't enough to dampen Justina's spirits as they took in the sights and sounds of the most fascinating place she had ever seen.

Unfortunately, a few hours later the three of them weren't quite so excited as they had first been when they had walked in the Forum. It was one thing to view its splendours from her bedroom window at the inn, but it was quite another when they had to push their way through the heaving mass of humanity that clogged the narrow streets as they'd somehow found their way into the *Subura*, the poor district of Rome. As none of them knew the city, they hadn't realised where they were heading, as they walked further away from the area around the Forum. It was only when Olivia had asked someone that they realised their mistake. They should have headed south, instead of east, as to the south they would have found the Velabrum, the general market, and the Forum Boarium and Forum Cuppedinis, where luxury goods could be bought.

But now, as the oppressive heat hit them, making it difficult to breath, Justina wished she'd had the foresight to ask the right way to the various markets. For a moment she had a pang of longing for the cooling winds that blew in off the Mediterranean back in Herculaneum.

But if the heat was bad, then the smells that assaulted her delicate nose were even worse! Everywhere they went the smell of raw sewage hit them. It was impossible to avoid as it flowed in open rivers down the streets. It had gotten so bad that the smell had very nearly caused Justina to bring up the meagre breakfast she'd had that morning.

"Ugh!" Olivia cried, as she shook off the filth that clung to the bottom of her dress. "This is disgusting!"

Justina agreed with her, and finally, having enough of the crowds, they turned back to the inn. Eventually, with the aid of Diogenes, who acted like a human battering ram, they made their way back to the Forum and the sanctuary of the inn. Hot, dirty and sweaty, Justina asked the innkeeper for a drink for all three of them, and taking pity on the dishevelled group, the inn keeper told them that there was a relaxing courtyard at the back of the inn where they might enjoy their drink in peace.

Justina paid for the drinks and thanked the innkeeper, making their way outside to sit down at one of several wooden tables that were scattered around a central fountain. Justina finally relaxed, taking in the quiet ambience of the courtyard, thinking how pleasant it was just to be able to breathe clean air!

Once she had recovered, she glanced around to see several other people, couples mainly, making the most of the relative peace of the courtyard.

Her eye caught an older woman, who was seated across from her, and the woman smiled at her. Justina reciprocated, before she broke eye contact and took another sip of her honey water.

"Mistress, I hope you do not mind my intrusion."

The words were spoken a few minutes later by the older woman, who had smiled across at her earlier.

"No. Not at all. What can I do for you?" Justina said, her tone friendly as she looked up to see the woman standing next to her.

"Well, it is more what I can do for you really." At Justina's frown, she pointed down at the hem of Justina's dress. "I could not help but see that it is ripped quite badly."

Justina gasped when she saw that the woman was right. She must have torn it when she had walked down the dirty, uneven streets. With hindsight she should never have worn the dress, as it was her best one.

"I am a seamstress. A good one, I like to think. I could repair it for you if you like."

For a moment Justina was undecided. She knew that Olivia's skills at needlework were not good, she had admitted that it was the one chore she hated; and Justina didn't have a clue as to how to repair the torn silk...

"I have a shop nearby," the woman interrupted, by way of explanation, "You could come there and one of my girls will mend it in next to no time."

Although she hadn't much experience with people, Justina knew instantly that this woman could be trusted, so she nodded, making her mind up, "That is very kind of you. If you don't mind I would be most grateful. "

A few minutes later the woman, whose name was Niobe, led the way out of the inn and headed for her shop with Justina, Olivia and Diogenes in attendance. It turned out that Niobe was the sister of the inn keeper, and had been visiting her brother and his family for a few hours before returning to her shop; and true to her words her dress shop was only a few minutes away from the Forum.

Once they entered the shop, which was split over two levels, the ground floor given over to the show room and dressing rooms, whilst on the first floor the seamstresses worked their magic, creating what appeared to be fabulous gowns of silk in all colours. Niobe told Justina to wait for a few moments whilst she sorted a few things out. As Justina looked around in amazement, she could see dozens and dozens of dresses hanging from every available space on the wall, and around twenty slaves busily working away. It was instantly obvious to Justina that this was no ordinary dressmakers, but one that must cater to the rich *patricians* of Rome.

Once Niobe had finished her business, she ushered Justina into one of her back rooms so that she could disrobe, providing her with a temporary shift whilst her dress was taken away by one of the slaves to be mended.

"You seem to have a thriving business here," she said a few moments later, once she had sat down on one of the couches provided for Niobe's rich clients.

"Too much work really," Niobe replied, "I cater for some rich *patricians*, but most of my dresses sell to the wives of the merchants who work in, and around, the Forum."

Her voice held a hint of pride, and Justina smiled at her, "Then I am even more grateful that you can spare the time to mend my dress."

"It is nothing. The gown is lovely, and it seemed a shame to see it spoiled so. I have a thing about silk. I hate to see it ripped, and when I do I have an uncontrollable urge to repair it!"

Justina laughed, relaxing in the woman's company and for a few moments a companionable silence fell between them, allowing Justina to finish off the goblet of honey water that had been provided for her when she had entered the shop.

After what could only have been a few minutes, the slave who had taken the dress away returned, and with a slight bow handed it back over to Justina. Glancing down at where the rip had been she could see that it had been repaired perfectly and now looked like new. There was no trace of the tear to be seen anywhere.

"Thank you so much. I am most grateful, it was my best dress." Justina said a few minutes later, after she had dressed and was once more in the front of the shop. Nodding slightly at Diogenes, he came over, and handed her a small purse of her money.

But before she could take out any money Niobe lifted her hand, "No charge. I insist. Call it part of the service. Maybe the next time you are in Rome and in need of a dress, you'll remember my shop?"

Justina was taken aback at her kindness and impulsively went over and hugged the woman, "Oh thank you so much! And yes, if ever I am need of a dress you will be the first person I will come to!"

* * *

The next day Justina arrived at the magnificent Circus Maximus. As she walked into the massive arena she was told by one of the attendants that Marsallas was not there, but that she was expected. As she followed the attendant – Diogenes and Olivia following in her wake – she couldn't help the pang of disappointment she felt when she realised that Marsallas wasn't going to be there.

But then why should he? She berated herself silently. As far as Marsallas was concerned, she was here to draw his horses and his chariot, not him. Eventually, they were escorted into Marsallas's quarters and she was told that Fabius Rufus would be arriving shortly to see to her needs.

True to the attendant's words the door opened a short while later, and Fabius Rufus walked towards her, a warm smile on his face. Seeing the younger man instantly reminded her of the day she had begged him to secure her an audience with Marsallas, and the memory of those events caused Justina's stomach to twist, and she was unable to stop the flush of colour that coloured her face as she remembered *all* that had happened that fateful day.

Fabius Rufus bowed slightly in greeting before saying, "Marsallas has been summoned to attend to Senator Lucius Apronius. The Senator sent a messenger here this morning requesting that

Marsallas go to his villa on the Palatine Hill as soon as possible. The Senator is one of our very generous benefactors, and he is, I understand, the man responsible for commissioning the statue you are making of Marsallas."

Justina took his hand in greeting, thankful that the younger man was far too polite to mention anything of what had happened between her and Marsallas, and she felt herself relax at his easy-going attitude *and* his explanation as to where Marsallas was. At least she now knew he wasn't avoiding her on purpose!

Once the introductions had been completed and Justina had declined a drink of honey water, Fabius set about showing her where Marsallas's horses and chariot were kept.

"I think I will draw the horses first. After that, would it be possible to take the chariot outside so I can see it in the daylight? The dimness of the store room would make it difficult to draw."

Fabius nodded. "That is no problem. I will bring the chariot out presently and set it in the arena itself. You can draw it quite easily if you sit in one of the stands."

* * *

Which was where Marsallas found her several hours later, in what was becoming her familiar pose – head bent over her parchment paper – her charcoal stick flying over the paper.

"You will burn in this sun if you stay out much longer."

Marsallas's amused tone startled Justina and she looked up to see him standing slightly behind her, annoyed and amazed at the same time that he always managed to creep up on her unannounced. For such a large man he was remarkably light-footed!

She lifted a hand to the nape of her neck feeling the sweat, unaware up until then, as to how hot it was in the arena. "I hadn't realised," she murmured, before lifting the papyrus paper up for him to see, "As you can see I've nearly finished. Ten more minutes or so."

"Good. No longer than that. I'll see you back in my quarters when you have finished." He bid her farewell with a slight bow, and Justina watched him walk away, admiring the strength of him, the powerful way he walked, her eyes taking in everything about him.

True to her word she finished her drawing within the allotted time, and made her way to Marsallas's quarters. As she stepped into the room she couldn't help the shiver of awareness that assailed her as she remembered the last time she'd been here in the room with him. Remembered the way he had kissed her, caressed her—

"Would you like a drink?"

The words jolted her out of her erotic memories, and she couldn't help the flush of colour that crept into her cheeks. Hoping he would take the colour in her cheeks for sunburn, she nodded, "Yes please. A glass of honey water would be lovely," and she was thankful when he turned away to pour her the drink.

"Did Fabius tell you where I have been this morning?" he asked, as he handed her a goblet of honey water.

"Yes. To Senator Lucius Apronius's villa, I understand."

"Umm, he found out that you are here and wants to meet with you." Marsallas's mouth twisted in wry humour, when he saw her surprised expression, "Don't ask me *how* he knows, Justina. He just does! Powerful men like Senator Lucius Apronius seem to know everything!" He gave her a knowing look, "He is holding a gathering at his villa tonight and we have been invited to attend."

"Me! Us!" Justina exclaimed, totally taken aback by the invitation. Then without thinking she blurted out, "But I don't have anything to wear."

Marsallas laughed, his teeth a stark white against the tanned skin of his face, and he shook his head in mock exasperation, "Typical female."

* * *

"So you see my dilemma?"

134

"Indeed I do. Indeed I do. Now come in and let's see what we can do."

Justina smiled a brilliant smile at Niobe, who, if surprised to see the younger woman return to her shop so soon, didn't say so.

"I think I have the ideal gown for you, as it happens. I made it recently, but the woman who ordered it has left Rome." She shrugged slightly, "I don't know why, but the rumours are rife that she is pregnant, and has left to visit an 'aunt' in Baiae to await the birth of the child!"

A few minutes later Justina found herself draped in a beautiful *stola* made of the lightest of silk, the colour of silver, with silver threads shot through it, so that when she turned the light reflected off it in shimmering waves.

"I have never seen such a beautiful gown," Justina whispered, overawed by the sheer loveliness of it. "Can I afford it?" She asked hesitantly, looking up at Niobe with doubt in her eyes.

"The dress is yours. It looks wonderful on you. Take it as a gift."

"But I can't—"

"Yes you can," Niobe interrupted, smiling at the shocked expression on Justina's face.

"The dress was languishing here in my shop doing nothing. Tonight you will wear it at a prestigious event. The way I see it, it will be the best advertisement I could ever hope for to have one of my dresses seen in the company of the rich *patricians* – Senator's wives no less! And of course if anyone asks you who made it, then I would be pleased if you could mention my name and where my shop is!"

At Niobe's genuine smile, Justina felt tears coming to her eyes. "You are so kind, Niobe, so kind. And it will be my honour to mention to others where your dress came from."

Justina left the shop half an hour later, with Olivia carrying not only the *stola*, but a silk *palla* – the cloak once again made of the finest material Justina had ever seen, a beautiful sea-green colour that Niobe was adamant would complement her grey eyes and dark hair.

Niobe had even managed to arrange for a new pair of sandals to be made, having sent one of her seamstresses to a shoemaker she knew in the Argiletum district of where all the shoe shops were apparently. The seamstress arrived back a short while later saying that Justina's sandals would be ready by the eleventh hour and would be delivered to her at the inn!

It was only when she was back in her bedroom at the inn, with Olivia fussing over her hair as she used a *calmistrum* – a hollow iron instrument in the shape of a rod to obtain lasting curls – that Justina realised how kind Niobe had been to her. She knew she was a good businesswoman, but that didn't detract from the kindness that she had shown her the first time she had seen her, yesterday afternoon, when she'd offered to mend her torn dress. Justina, so taken aback by everything that had happened, had only just realised that the sandals that had arrived half an hour ago had also been paid for by Niobe, Justina having completely forgotten to pay for them! Mortified she had sent Diogenes back to the shop with some money for them, but once again Justina was touched by Niobe's generosity, as she hadn't even mentioned the cost of the sandals previously.

"None of the women Niobe has working for her are slaves, you know."

Justina shook her thoughts away, focusing on what Olivia was saying. Then as the words sunk in Justina gasped slightly at what the younger girl was saying, "Really? But how do you know?"

Olivia smiled, "One of her seamstresses told me. She has freed all her slaves and pays them a good wage to work for her. She doesn't believe in slavery, apparently, says it's an abomination. It goes without saying that all the women working for her love her!"

Justina turned to look at Olivia, and as one, both women smiled at each other, as they realised how incredibly lucky they were to have been touched by Niobe's kindness. But as Olivia's words sunk in she couldn't help wondering if there was more to Niobe that just kindness. She thought of Lydia and her family, of *their* kindness, and *their* abhorrence of slavery, and wondered if Niobe was a Christian just like them...

CHAPTER FOURTEEN

Marsallas watched as Justina came towards him as he stood waiting for her outside the inn.

Inwardly, he took a deep breath at the picture of loveliness she presented. In the fading daylight, he could see that she wore a silver *stola* of the finest silk that moulded her body, hinting at the curves beneath as it clung to her. In her arms she carried a *palla*, as the evening was far too warm for the cloak at the moment.

But it was her hair that drew his eyes. It had been artfully arranged in an elaborate style, no doubt by her tire-woman, Olivia. The girl had done her proud, as one fat curl fell either side of her face highlighting the paleness of her ivory skin. The rest of her hair had been piled up on top of her head, and Marsallas could see that ivory and tortoiseshell combs had been used to keep it in place. She looked every inch the rich *patrician*, and Marsallas could not hold back the feeling of desire that surged through him as she walked towards him.

He wanted to kiss her, ravish her, take her to his bed and make her beg for him. Only he couldn't do that, of course, as Senator Apronius was waiting for them.

"You look lovely," he whispered, as she came to stand next to him, "All the men will be jealous of me for having such a beautiful companion tonight." He inhaled her fragrance. A fragrance that was uniquely hers, and he imagined trailing his lips over her sensitive warm skin, licking, lapping all the secret places of her body until she went mindless with wanting him.

Justina looked up at him and smiled, "Truly? Because at this very moment I am so scared my insides are churning like mad."

Marsallas laughed, but he could see her nervousness reflected in the darkness of her eyes at what lay ahead of her tonight. "Be yourself, Justina, and everyone will be enchanted, trust me."

* * *

"Close your mouth, you're gaping like a fish!"

Justina eyes snapped back to his, and she smiled, "I am aren't I? But I have never seen such a splendid villa. It is amazing! I swear that is an authentic marble sculpture by Polyclitus's own hands!"

Marsallas looked over to where Justina was pointing at a sculpture, the head of an Amazon that was displayed prominently in the *vestibulum*.

As they followed one of Senators slaves through the villa, he could see that Justina was totally mesmerised by the sumptuous villa. Senator Lucius Apronius was a great patron of the arts, and this was reflected in the sheer amount of artwork he had accumulated over the years. Although he had been to the Senator's villa on many occasions he could now see, that to someone like Justina, an artist in her own right, just how wonderful it all was.

As they walked through the finely decorated rooms, with their myriad wall hangings and paintings, that seemed to cover every available space right up to the vast ceilings hung with their copper rafters, Marsallas could now appreciate it from Justina's point of view. The wall hangings, paintings, sculptures depicting the gods such as Pan, Apollo, the Golden Cupids, and paintings of the Trojan Wars were the best money could buy.

And the villa itself was a work of art in its own way! It boasted five reception rooms, each one more elaborately decorated than the last. The *atrium* had the most amazing ornamental pond, reputedly the largest in Rome, and the rainwater that fed it came via the opening in the roof where there was a *compluvium* – rain collector – which sloped inwards to the ornamental pond.

Marsallas knew that off the *atrium* there were the lavishly furnished guest bedrooms – the *cubicula* – with beds made of the finest woods, decorated with ivory and bronze, as he had stayed in them on many occasions.

* * *

As they were taken through the *peristylium* the first thing Justina saw was a magical array of sparkling fountains. To the rear was a leafy half-courtyard of ornamental hedges of boxwood, and more fine statues were placed along the hedgerow.

Justina couldn't resist, and she quickly walked over to them, touching one of them, running her hands over the bronze, amazed by the craftsmanship. It was only when she heard someone shout Marsallas's name in greeting that she stopped what she was doing and turned away from the sculpture to see a tall thin man of indeterminate age walking towards them, attired in his Senator's toga.

"Welcome, welcome, welcome," he boomed at them, taking hold of Justina's hands as soon as he came within touching distance, "Welcome to my humble home."

Justina had to bite back the giggle that threatened, as she looked into his twinkling eyes.

"I can see why Marsallas wants you to sculpt him, *and* keep you to himself, you are very beautiful," he said, bending over to kiss her hand, before leading her into the dining room.

As they entered the *triclinium*, Justina tensed slightly when she saw that it was already full, and it seemed as if everybody stopped talking at once, turning to stare at them as they walked in. Trying to quell the nerves that threatened, she was relieved when the kindly Senator patted her hand, "It will be fine, my dear. Just relax, we are simple folk, that is all."

This time Justina couldn't hold back the giggle that escaped, and looked across at him, seeing that he was smiling at her, a fond expression on his face.

They were escorted to a couch, and Justina realised that she was to lie next to Marsallas and the Senator. As was the Roman tradition, there was a central table with an arrangement of three couches to lie on while dining. The fourth side of the table was open, so the slaves could attend to them and serve the food.

"Did you know we are – *locus consulars* – the guests of honour?" Marsallas whispered as they made themselves comfortable on the couch.

"Are we?" she whispered back, pleased to see the relaxed expression on his face. She fought back her feelings, as she took in how handsome he looked tonight. Gone was the normal veneer of hardness that surrounded him. Tonight his face was relaxed, a small smile playing at the side of his mouth. He was dressed in a tunic of dark-blue silk, the colour a perfect foil for his eyes and his dark hair.

"Yes we are. The seating arrangements are very precise at these types of gatherings. The fact that we are lying with the Senator is causing much talk amongst the other guests."

Justina hadn't realised the significance of lying next to the Senator, but when she glanced around she saw that all the other guests were watching them covertly.

All except one, and Justina couldn't contain the shiver that went through her when she met the fierce gaze of one woman seated across from her. Her eyes were trained on her with such ferocity that Justina blinked rapidly, resisting the strange urge to look behind her, to see if it was someone *else* who was the target of her venom.

But she knew there was no one behind her, and in an unconscious gesture Justina lifted her chin in an unspoken challenge. If anything, the woman's eyes narrowed even further at Justina's gesture, but then, as if suddenly bored with her, the woman curled her lip in disdain and turned her regal head away.

Justina was at a loss as to why she had been the victim of her censure. The woman was around her age, incredibly beautiful and poised, and dressed, as would be expected, in a gown of the finest silk, the colour of ripe oranges, adorned with pearls and other semi-precious jewels. The clasps securing her dress at the shoulders were gold, again encrusted with jewels, and the whole outfit was a perfect foil for her auburn hair.

Justina watched as the woman leaned across to a handsome man who lay beside her, her hand stroking his arm in a familiar gesture, before whispering something in his ear. The man laughed and looked over at Justina. Hot colour flooded her face when she realised that the woman must have said something derogatory about her, and she turned away, her heart beating fast.

"Don't mind them, my dear."

She turned to see Senator Lucius Apronius smiling kindly at her.

"They are just jealous. The rich of Rome have nothing else to do but gossip and hate anyone who dares to stand in their way."

"But I haven't done anything." Justina protested weakly.

"Yes you have. Firstly, you are lying next to me, and secondly you are lying next to Marsallas," he paused, "But thirdly, and most importantly, you are beautiful and gifted."

If anything, Justina blushed even more, and the Senator laughed out loud, patting her hand in consolation. "Now enough of petty politics, tell me how you came to be such a good sculptress?"

* * *

"Are you enjoying yourself?" Marsallas asked.

"Oh yes, the acrobats were amazing. I've never seen the like before."

"Umm. They were good weren't they?" Then he leaned forward and whispered, "Have I told you how beautiful you look tonight?"

The words caused Justina's heart to thump against her breastbone, and she sat transfixed, conscious of the passion she could see deep in his eyes.

"You're beautiful as well," she said, the words tumbling out.

Marsallas laughed out loud at her words, "Men aren't beautiful, Justina."

Justina stiffened and she turned flashing eyes to his, "Of course they are!" she said heatedly, "As a sculptress I can tell you that a man's body can be as beautiful as any woman's. The muscularity of a man is a delight to sculpt. Why do think that there are more sculptures of men than women?"

Marsallas lifted a hand in supplication, "Stop!" he said smiling at her, "I understand what you are saying, and I take it all back. You are right, of course. Men's bodies can be beautiful," and before Justina could reply, Marsallas leaned in even closer, his breath warm as it feathered against the nape of her neck, causing her to shiver in response, loving the male musky scent of him as he leaned over her, "I never knew you could be so passionate, Justina. I hope to see your passion for myself one day."

Heat pooled in her stomach at his words, at the intensity of his gaze and the moment was only broken when a trumpeter heralded the start of the evening meal. The doors to the *triclinium* were flung open, as slave after slave entered, carrying gold platters piled high with food.

As expected, the meal was sumptuous; simple food such as honey cakes and dates competed with gastronomic delights such as honey-roast fowl, broad beans cooked with cumin and coriander, suckling pig stuffed with sausage meat. There were even snails and the delicate flesh of thrushes and other song birds to eat, as well as the great delicacy of stuffed door mice.

Even the desserts were nothing like she had ever tasted. Along with dishes of fresh, and dried fruit, seasoned with pepper to bring out the coolness of the fruit, there was ice cream. How the Senator had managed to get ice cream to a hot, humid city like

Rome she would never know, but the ice cream, whose base was made from snow, must have somehow been transported from the distant mountains.

"What did you think of the food?"

Justina groaned theatrically, "I've never eaten so much in all my life. If I ate like that every day, I would soon become too fat to move!"

Marsallas laughed, "I am just thankful that I do a lot of exercise," Marsallas said, patting his flat muscular stomach. Then he got up off the couch and stood up, holding his hand out to her, "Shall we? The Senator has arranged some entertainment in the *peristylium* I understand."

Justina stood up and placed her hand in his, aware of the warmth of him, the strength of him, as his large hand engulfed her much smaller one as he led her out into the colonnaded garden. Once more she couldn't contain the shiver of desire that hit her when she caught the smell of sandalwood coming off his skin, and she had the urge to run her hands over—

"I understand the show is out of this world."

The words jolted Justina out of her own fantasy world, and she berated herself for letting her mind wander so. But it was awfully difficult to concentrate when his skin touched hers, making her aware of him all the time.

Once they were settled, sitting on high-backed chairs made of bronze and upholstered in the softest of silk, the show began. A play acted out, not by human actors, she saw in amazement, but by a mechanical cast – a circle of dancing puppets – who moved in perfect harmony and animated the world around them into plumes of fire and fountains of milk. Justina had never seen anything like it in her life, and as she looked around at her fellow guests, she could see that even the most jaded in the audience gaped open-mouthed at these new wonders.

"They are made by Heron of Alexandria apparently," Marsallas whispered in her ear.

Justina had never heard of Heron of Alexandria, but she didn't care! The metal puppets were magnificent, and she watched the show mesmerised, totally enthralled.

"Would you like a drink?" Marsallas asked, a while later.

Justina nodded, not for a moment taking her eyes off the show, only vaguely aware of Marsallas leaving her as he went in search of some refreshment for her.

"So you are the mysterious, Justina."

The words were spoken behind her, a few minutes later, and Justina turned in her chair to see the woman who had been staring at her earlier, looking down at her, her eyes full of malice. For a moment Justina was taken aback at how beautiful the woman was. Up close, she could see the perfection of her face and eyes clearly. Eyes that were an amazing green colour, slanted like a cats, and expertly made up with dark eyeliner like some Egyptian queen. The rest of her face was perfection as well, having been made up with powders and paints designed to emphasise her delicate features.

"Have you become Marsallas's lover yet?"

Justina stiffened at her words, her chin rising slightly in anger, "I don't see what business it is of yours—"

The woman laughed harshly, cutting off Justina's words, "Well, well, well, an innocent no less!" She paused for a moment, letting her words sink in, her eyes even colder than before, "I thought as much when I first saw you. How naughty of Marsallas to tease me so."

Justina was just about to say once again that it was none of her business, when the woman lifted her hand, "But I am being remiss, let me explain. It *is* my business you see. Marsallas is my lover." She paused slightly, letting her words sink in, "I don't mind sharing him of course, we have a fluid relationship so to speak, but I'm sure he has told you that."

Justina felt the colour drain from her face, and it was all the other woman needed to see to deliver her final blow, "Now don't distress yourself my dear," she said patting her shoulder in a false display of sympathy, "Enjoy him while you can, he is a superb lover, *I* can vouch for that. Just don't be surprised when he comes back to me. He always does. None of his other women last for long."

And with that, she walked past Justina, her head held high, her stride confident, the sway of her hips designed to entice any man that cared to look as she walked past.

* * *

"You seem to be enjoying yourself this evening, Marsallas."

Marsallas turned away from the table, "Claudetta," he acknowledged by way of greeting, deliberately ignoring her comment. His only reaction to it, and the sarcastic tone that it had been delivered in, was the slight tightening of his hands that held the two goblets of wine he'd just picked up.

"May I?" She asked, nodding at one of the goblets.

Marsallas pursed his lips in annoyance, but said nothing as he handed one over to her.

"Thank you, darling," she purred, looking up at him from under her long lashes, the movement one she was well versed in, and one he'd seen played out a hundred times before.

It was a gesture designed to maximise her allure towards men, but it was one he'd quickly grown tired of, and it now irritated him to the point of anger. He took a sip of his wine, and reigned in his temper before saying cordially, "I'm not your '*darling*' any more, Claudetta, I thought we had already established that." He took a small measure of satisfaction when he saw her eyes narrow, and before she could say anything he remarked, "Besides, I saw you with Atticus earlier. I understand he's your latest lover."

Claudetta made a moue with her mouth, "Are you jealous, darl- Marsallas?"

Marsallas's mouth twisted in derision, but he delayed in answering her by taking another sip of his wine as he took his measure of her. He knew Claudetta of old. She was definitely in

146

one of her trouble-making moods, he would bet his last *sesterce* on it. Finally he answered her, "No, far from it," and he took a small amount of pleasure when he saw her eyes darken in anger as his words hit home.

But she quickly masked her reaction, and emulating him by taking a small sip of her wine, "Umm. So I saw. You seem besotted with your little sculptress," and before Marsallas could say anything she laughed lightly, "And I can see why. She is charming, quite the innocent—"

"What did you say to her, Claudetta?" he bit out, not bothering to hide his anger this time. He cursed himself for being a fool for leaving Justina alone. There was no stopping someone like Claudetta when she had her claws out.

Claudetta lifted one expertly plucked eyebrow, "Oh, you know, girl talk. This and that," then she paused dramatically before whispering, "Your prowess as a lover and the fact that I don't mind sharing you…"

"Bitch," Marsallas said through gritted teeth.

Claudetta laughed falsely, "Always darling. Always," and her hand reached out, as fast as a striking snake, to stroke a slim finger down his cheek, before her eyes flitted to a point behind Marsallas's left shoulder. "Oops," she murmured, smiling brightly, "I think we've just been caught."

Marsallas stepped back from her and whipped his head around to see Justina standing in the doorway. Her face was ashen, her eyes wide with shock and disappointment as she watched the byplay between him and Claudetta.

"Shit," he hissed, as their eyes clashed across the room. Hers were the first to drop away before she turned and fled.

* * *

A few minutes later he found her leaning against one of the marble columns that formed part of the huge doorway to the villa. Her

147

palla was draped over her shoulders to ward off the chill of the night air.

"There is to be another show—" But he stopped speaking abruptly when he saw her stiffen and turn towards him, her eyes flashing anger at him as he approached. The cordial atmosphere that had existed between them earlier that evening had now been replaced by suspicion and mistrust on her part.

Curse Claudetta and her interfering ways. Annoyance surged through him as he realised that Justina had obviously believed *everything* that Claudetta had told her without question. If she had *bothered* to ask him what- He cut off his wayward thoughts abruptly. What did it matter what she thought about him? She was to be his mistress, nothing more, nothing less. All he wanted from her was one night of her body, as he'd demanded. *Then* he would discard her, as she had discarded him—

"I would like to leave if that is possible."

Her voice was pure ice as she cut him off, and Marsallas stiffened as frustration ate at him.

"As you wish," he said harshly, bitterness coating his tongue. "I have several races tomorrow afternoon. Diogenes will take you back to the farm tomorrow morning." Then he beckoned to one of the slaves who stood nearby, and in a matter of seconds the huge door was opened and they stepped out into the night.

* * *

The journey back to the inn was undertaken in complete silence, and as soon as they arrived, Marsallas jumped out of the sedan chair and waited for her to get out, holding out his hand to help her. He saw her hesitate for a moment, undecided as to whether to take it or not, but after a moment's deliberation she placed her hand in his.

Again Marsallas felt a surge of annoyance flow through him when he saw her hesitation, and he bit back his anger, the only outward sign of it a nerve that he felt pulsing in the hard set of his jaw. He led her into the hallway, only stopping when he reached the bottom of the staircase that led up to her room. Justina went to pull away from him, but he tightened his grip slightly, stopping her. Her eyes flashed their annoyance up at him, but he ignored it. Then, in a deliberate movement he leaned forward, taking a small amount of pleasure when he saw the anger in her eyes give way to wariness. *Good.* Finally, he had managed to elicit a response out of her, and he smiled in satisfaction.

"Just so you know *all* the facts, Justina," he said in a soft voice, before he made a fist with his free hand and raised a finger, "*One.* Don't believe everything you see." With a slight tug of his hand he brought her closer, watching as her eyes widened slightly at the unexpectedness of it. Then he lifted a second finger, "*Two.* Claudetta is a first-rate bitch who would eat the likes of you for breakfast," again another tug of his hand forced her closer, and he took a small perverse sense of satisfaction in that she was now totally at his mercy, "And *three,*" a third, and final finger, joined the other two, "Claudetta *was* my lover, but she isn't any more. I haven't bedded her in over six months, and I have no intention of ever doing so again."

A third, and final, tug pulled her fully into the hard length of his body, and he felt her surrender to him, as the anger and mistrust finally left her eyes, to be replaced with desire. Taking advantage, he bent his head and kissed her. It was a soft kiss, one designed to lull, to comfort, and it had the desired effect when he saw her eyes flutter shut. But then, deliberately, he pulled away, putting some much-needed distance between her soft body and his own pulsing one. He took satisfaction in the fact that her eyes now registered disappointment.

"Sweet dreams, Justina." And with a mocking salute he left her standing there.

CHAPTER FIFTEEN

Justina watched him walk over to the small building, just as he'd done every night for the past week since he'd finally returned to the villa. *Had it been a whole month since that disastrous evening at Senator Apronius's villa?*

She knew where he went; he'd shown her the bath house when she had first arrived at the villa. It was his pride and joy, a small-scale version of the baths he frequented when in Rome. There were mirrors of polished bronze covering the walls and ceiling, and a pool lined with rich marble. A miniature hypocaust, a complex system of pipes and conduits, fed the bath house with hot steam keeping everything piping hot, no matter the time of day or the outside weather.

As she sat on the window ledge, in what was becoming her nightly routine since his arrival, Justina frowned in frustration as he closed the door to the bathhouse behind him. It was as if he were playing some kind of game with her. And it had been like that ever since he'd arrived back at the villa.

His attitude was unusual, to say the least. Instead of being cool, even angry, with her, after he'd left her at the inn back in Rome, he had, in fact, been the complete opposite. Cordial, amenable, the epitome of politeness whenever he spoke to her, or enquired about the progress of the bronze. Yes, she mused to herself, he was *definitely* up to something, but she couldn't quite put her finger on, couldn't quite fathom out what he wanted.

What on earth was he playing at? She bit her lip in frustration, as her brain raced furiously. Then reality dawned like a bolt of lightning, and she thumped her hand on the marble window sill in vexation. *Oh how could she have been so stupid? Of course! He was waiting. Waiting for her to come to him! It was going to be her choice as to whether she would honour their bargain. It was going to be her decision, to take the final step, if you liked, as to whether she would make the first move and go to him for the one night he asked for.*

Relief surged through her, "Yes," she breathed, as she stared out across the courtyard. "I will come to you, Marsallas."

Finally, after all these years, it was now time to bury the ghosts of their pasts. The six years of hurt and longing between the both of them would end this night – one way or another.

Slipping off the windowsill, Justina padded across her room, letting the moon, which had appeared from behind the clouds, guide her towards the door. She was just about to open the bedroom door when she hesitated for a moment. Turning, she went over to her bed and reached up behind her head, quickly removing the necklace she always wore, before placing it under her pillow for safe keeping.

The necklace was precious to her, she had worn it every day since her sixteenth birthday, and it held too many memories, memories that for the time being, she didn't want Marsallas to know about...

Once she had made sure that the necklace was safe, she finally left her room and headed for the bathhouse, where she knew Marsallas would be waiting for her...

* * *

The steam hit her as soon as she opened the door; the silk of her dress clinging to her body as the heat instantly saturated the fabric. She stood in the doorway, letting her eyes adjust to the dim interior. There were only two oil lamps illuminating the bathing area, and it took Justina several seconds to see Marsallas sitting in the water, his eyes closed as he leaned his head back against a marble column. He looked relaxed, and a shiver of longing went through her. She could see a *stirgyl*, and a jar of oil sitting on the marble tiles next to him, and it was obvious that he had recently oiled himself, as his skin glistened in the flickering light.

Justina took in the sight of him, his smooth, muscled chest, the powerful breadth of his shoulders, the corded muscles of his neck as he leaned back—

"Justina."

The words were said so softly that Justina started, and her eyes met his, seeing in an instant that he was watching her, a dark look on his face.

"At last." His voice was husky, as he slowly sat upright in the hot water, his eyes never leaving hers.

Justina watched mesmerised as water trailed over the smooth expanse of his chest, saw his nipples harden as they were exposed to cool air; and as if in response to the awakening desire she was feeling, she felt hers tighten too, pebbling under her gown into tight buds that pushed against the damp silk. She saw his eyes drop to them, as he too became aware of her body's involuntary response to him, and for a moment she had to resist the urge to lift her arms and cover herself. But she didn't, and instead she finally answered his question, "Yes, Marsallas. At last."

She heard his hiss and her heart accelerated when he stood up, revealing every inch of his gloriously naked body. She bit back a gasp, as her eyes travelled downwards, over the vast expanse of his chest, the flat ridges of muscle that bisected his stomach down to the fullness of his erection, standing proud at the juncture of his thighs. Her eyes snapped back to his face in wonder, only for her to swallow the lump of emotion in her throat, when she saw the desire in his eyes pierce her very core.

There was no going back now, she knew that, and without conscious thought she walked towards him, stopping only when she came to the steps at the edge of the pool. Marsallas lifted a hand in invitation, and Justina smiled, walking fully clothed into the pool, taking the outstretched hand that he offered.

She shivered with reaction as the wet warmth of his hand closed around hers, pulling her into the heat of his body; felt the friction of her gown against the hardness of the muscles of his chest, the pleasure that his touch elicited.

As she stood next to him, waist-deep in the water, he pulled her even closer into his hard body, and she was acutely aware of the fullness of his erection nestled in the warmth of her stomach. She arched into his body, his strong arms pulling her tight into his wet nakedness. Warm wet flesh met fabric, the thin silk of her gown moulding to her legs like a second skin, the smoothness of the material strangely erotic as it rubbed against her skin.

Marsallas leaned down and kissed her, his hands gripping the softness of her upper arms, pinning her to his body as the heat of his lips met the coolness of hers. There was no going back – even if she wanted to. The feelings that were pulsing through her were too real, too raw, keeping her captive as if she were chained to him.

Justina heard him growl deep in his throat, as his kiss deepened, his arms gripping hers, almost painful in their intensity, as they communicated his feeling for her. Warmth began to grow in her body as his hands moved down her back, over the curve of her hips and waist, feather-light caresses that moved upwards until they cupped her breasts, all the while never once breaking their kiss. Even through the thin fabric of her silk gown, his touch was overpowering her senses, her breasts swelling under his touch, the nipples hard and sensitive to every stroke of his fingers.

Eventually, his hands left her breasts to stroke upwards, to the softness of her flushed cheek, pushing a tendril of her dark hair away from her face, his fingers gentle as they moved over her skin, trailing down to the line of her jaw, her chin, the delicate skin of her neck. Justina's breath stopped in her chest, and she tried to swallow but couldn't, as she felt the gentleness of his touch.

His kiss deepened, becoming a long, slow exploration of pleasure, nipping, teasing all the while leaving her wanting more. One hand slid down, to cup her bottom, pulling her even closer, so that their bodies met, hip to hip, thigh to thigh, breast to breast, until she felt his hips move, thrusting against the softness of her lower belly, his hardness demanding a release. Warmth surged through her, a heavy lassitude of desire that threatened to overwhelm her.

"You're wearing too many clothes," he whispered, breaking off the kiss his breath feather soft against her lips.

"Yes."

The one word was enough, and Marsallas drew back slightly, reaching up with both hands to grasp the neck of her sodden gown. He tightened his fists in the folds and Justina heard the sound of silk ripping as he slowly tugged at the fabric, pulling it apart with ease, his movements so controlled that it was infinitely more sexual than if he had ripped it open with force. Slow inch, by slow agonising inch, her body was bared to him, until she stood naked in the water, his gaze taking in everything.

He bunched up the useless gown and threw it away, hissing though his teeth as his eyes took in the beauty of her naked body, the high points of her breasts, erect and aching with desire, down over the flatness of her stomach, and the gentle swell of her hips, lower, until his gaze took in the small triangle of dark hair at the apex of her thighs. She couldn't control her visible shudder as he took his fill of her.

His eyes snapped back to hers. Desire. Pure unadulterated desire flamed from his eyes as she looked up at him, and then he smiled before he leaned forward and traced a finger down the hollow between her breasts, taking a droplet of moisture from her skin before lifting his finger to his mouth, sucking at the wetness.

"Your turn," he whispered.

Emboldened by his seductive command, she bent towards him, her finger taking a droplet of water from his skin before she leaned forward and pressed soft kisses against his super-heated skin. The taste of him was so intense, so erotic, *so* real, that she never wanted the moment to end, and she gloried in the power she had over him as she felt his body jerk when she took his erect nipple in her mouth and bit it gently.

His hands traced the gentle swell of her hips, encircling them, breaking her hold over him for a moment, and before she could protest, Marsallas lifted her as if she weighed nothing; until her breasts were in direct alignment with his mouth. He took one full mound into his mouth, his expert tongue sucking, biting and kissing the sensitive aureole, until she whimpered in longing.

* * *

Marsallas smiled against the softness of her skin as he kissed her breast, delighting in the soft noises she was making. Placing a final kiss on the swollen nipple, he transferred his mouth to Justina's other breast, felt her back arch in wanton pleasure as she communicated her wants, her desires, to him without words.

After an eternity he finished his tortuous exploration of her breasts, but instead of letting her go, he lifted her higher, feeling her nails dig into the muscles of his shoulders, and this time his mouth trailed hot wet kisses over the wet skin of her abdomen, sipping at the droplets of water that flowed off her skin.

"M...Marsallas...I." Justina's words were incoherent, her head shaking from side to side with abandon, totally lost in the feelings his mouth was inflicting on her body.

"Shh, Justina. Let yourself go," he whispered against her belly, tasting her, the heat of her skin about to consume them both, until finally his mouth found the wet soft curls of her womanhood. His mouth covered her, and Justina arched in abandon. Eventually he stopped, pulling himself away, letting her body slide down over

155

his hard torso, past his full erection, until they were once again waist-deep in the water, facing each other.

He could hear her soft pants as she rested her head on his shoulder. Then he gently lifted her chin, making her meet his eyes, "There's no going back now, Justina, you know that don't you?"

Justina nodded, "I want you, Marsallas. I always have."

Marsallas's eyes darkened with passion at her words. So here it was. The moment of truth. What he'd been waiting for ever since he'd seen her in his quarters at the Circus, and he couldn't control the emotions he felt for her. He wanted her more now than when he'd been eighteen.

Momentarily, he ruthlessly pushed back the thought of her being with his uncle. That was the past. Here. Now. That was *all* that mattered. He was finally going to have what he had craved for years now.

"Good," he breathed, "Good." Then his lips swooped down, capturing her mouth, before he lifted her in his arms as if she weighed nothing, and waded through the hot water, her slim body cradled in his strong muscular arms as he walked up the steps and out of the bath.

* * *

The coldness of the night air was a sharp contrast to the heat of the steamy bath water, and Justina shivered as she was carried across the bath house until she felt herself being lowered onto a couch. Marsallas leaned over her, his arms braced either side of her head, his left knee resting on the edge of the silken couch, waiting, never once breaking eye contact with hers.

Her hand reached up to cup the back of his neck. The unspoken gesture communicated her need and spurred him on. "Yes," he hissed, as he lowered himself over her, their bodies fitting together as if they had been made for each other.

"I want you," he growled, his blue eyes darkened to almost

black by the intensity of his need. "Open yourself for me, Justina."

Justina did as he bid, her thighs parting to allow his hard body to settle over her softness, her arms reaching up to hold onto the hardness of his broad shoulders, her eyes closing as desire once more washed over her.

"Watch me. Open your eyes, Justina. I want you to see *me* when I enter you. I want you to know exactly *who* is above you."

Justina's eyes flew open at his words, but he ignored the hurt that he must have seen in her eyes as he slid into the heat of her body. But then he stopped, his body tensing and Justina knew that he must have felt the barrier of her virginity. She watched, mesmerised, as his head fell back, exposing the muscles of his throat, which convulsed with emotion, as he finally realised she had been telling the truth after all.

"No, no, no," he shouted up at the ceiling, his eyes pinched shut in pain, "It's not supposed to be like this." And then he tensed all the muscles of his arms, and with what must have been a super-human strength, he started to withdraw from her body.

"Please, Marsallas. Don't leave me," Justina whispered, when she realised what his intention was, "Please. I want this. I want *you*," her hands gripped his shoulders, trying desperately to bring him back. Then with a woman's instinct, she lifted her legs and wrapped them around Marsallas's waist, stopping his movements, before she angled her hips and pushed upwards with all her strength, joining her body fully with his. She was unable to stop the gasp of pain that shot through her. But thankfully the pain was fleeting. She could feel him inside her, his fullness finally completing her.

She felt victorious when Marsallas's head came to rest on the curve of her shoulder, felt him shudder uncontrollably, his breath hot and heavy on her neck as he lay still in her embrace. Emboldened, she lifted her hands and smoothed them down the tense muscles of his back, lower until they gripped the smoothness of his buttocks.

"Ahh, Justina," he groaned, her touch obviously enough to

reignite his passion. Then she felt him move, as if he were power-less to stop the surging demands of his body. Eventually he lifted his head from her shoulder to take her lips once more, and her lips parted eagerly, giving him full access. Justina never imagined that a kiss could be so powerful, as his mouth slanted over hers, his tongue delving between her lips, searching, teasing, finding her tongue, mating with her, fencing, retreating, only to plunge once more into her moist depth. She arched as his fingers encircled her throat, her body trembling with reaction as his hips pounded into her body.

Then he stilled, their bodies intimately joined, before his lips finally broke away from hers to trail down over her throat, his mouth skimming over her sensitive skin, planting hot wet kisses on the curve of her neck, until, like a starving man they once again found the softness of her mouth, the kiss so deep that she convulsed around him, and she heard him groan, before his hips moved once more with a rhythm that was as old as time, the friction so intense that it was only a matter of seconds before she arched in ecstasy as her orgasm ripped through her. It was enough to finally send him over the edge and she felt his body pulse, his seed spilling deep inside her, his voice loud and hoarse in the stillness of the night as he shouted out his release.

* * *

Languor seeped into her bones. She could feel him inside her, still joined intimately as only a man and a woman could be; content to listen to the deep, steady beat of his heart, his arms wrapped around her protectively. It felt so right to be in his arms. At last.

He moved slightly, and she lifted her head up to look at him. Her stomach quivered when she saw the closed expression on his face.

"You should have stopped me."

"I didn't want you to stop."

"So you told the truth after all. And I didn't believe you."

Justina heard the tinge of bitterness, of regret, in his voice. "It doesn't matter." She lifted her hand and ran it through his hair, glorying in the texture. Her hand stilled, and she asked hesitantly, "Would you have made love to me if you *had* believed me?"

She heard Marsallas's deep sigh, and after a long pause he answered, "I'm not sure."

Justina shifted slightly, her body closing around him, squeezing him, and she smiled slightly when she heard his groan of pleasure.

"Are you sure you don't know, Marsallas?" she asked softly, when she felt him harden inside her once again.

She heard him grunt at the pleasure her body was giving to his. Then she couldn't stop the squeal of fright when he swung his legs off the couch and sat up, with her still intimately joined with him, before he stood up. Instinctively, she wrapped her legs around his waist, her head cradled against his neck and shoulder as he walked towards the hot pool once more.

"What are you doing?" she whispered, her head lolling back to look at him.

Marsallas laughed softly, "You do ask silly questions, Justina," then he leaned forward and kissed her.

CHAPTER SIXTEEN

Marsallas stared sightlessly at the ceiling, his arms folded behind his head as he watched the rising sun chase the night shadows away. How long he had been awake he didn't know, but it must have been hours.

He was acutely aware of Justina sleeping next to him, and his lips twisted in derision as he acknowledged to himself that for the first time in his adult life, he had *actually* allowed a woman to spend the night with him. And how ironic that it was the *one* woman who had plagued his thoughts both day, and night, for years.

Marsallas's teeth clenched, biting into his jaw, frustration clawing at him. For six long years he had imposed an iron will over his emotions. He had been immune to feminine wiles, refusing to allow any woman to control him. Many had tried. Claudetta had been the last, and she'd soon learned that he was no woman's plaything.

Perhaps he'd been too long without a woman. He'd been celibate for over six months, preferring to put all his energies into being the best charioteer that he could, as well as building up his olive-oil business. And, if he were honest with himself, since Justina had come back into his life, his only consuming thought had been his revenge, his "plan" for her. A plan which, he now acknowledged with a wry twist of his lips, lay in tatters.

And strangely, irrationally, he also felt angry.

Angry that Justina had been a virgin. Angry that she'd obviously lied to him about wanting to be with his uncle. Angry that he'd let a woman finally get under his skin, but most importantly of all, angry that he'd wasted so many years hating her. He sighed deeply, finally acknowledging to himself that he had never wanted any woman as much as he had wanted Justina.

* * *

Justina stirred, waking slowly, stretching out her long legs as she lay curled on her side.

She smiled to herself as she recalled that she had just been having the most delicious dream. She'd been imagining her fingers threading through the thickness of Marsallas's hair. Waking him up slowly with the rhythmic stroking. Would he be angry if she trailed her finger over the hard planes of his face? Would he welcome the touch of her fingers on the smoothness of his chest? Lower…and she had the sudden compulsion to test out her questions.

She lifted a hand to push back her tangled hair, and as she did so her arm encountered warm hard flesh. She froze, and her eyes sprang open and she met Marsallas's hooded gaze. Like her, he was lying on his side, a hand propping up his head. Watching. Waiting. Waiting for her to wake, and her heart squeezed into a painful knot. Here it was – the morning after the night before.

She looked away quickly, noting with a slight start that she was in his bedchamber. Her eyes took in the masculine furniture, his wooden chest where he kept his clothes, the dark tapestry that hung on the wall. A remarkably Spartan room for such a wealthy man.

And a room she didn't even remember him carrying her into. She had been so wrapped up in their lovemaking last night, she hadn't even noticed that he'd brought her here. *That* thought prompted a blush that started from the tips of her toes right to the top of her head—

"Good morning, Justina."

The simple greeting, delivered in a mocking tone, made her stiffen. But refusing to be cowed, she turned and met his eyes once more. "It is for me. But I'm not sure if it is for you."

He raised an eyebrow, his face darkening slightly. "Maybe you would like to tell me how you were still a virgin – well up until last night, anyway."

Justina stiffened at his supercilious tone, and sat up, pulling the thin silk covering over her nakedness. "I would have thought it obvious really. Your uncle didn't want me." He snorted in derision, "Somehow I can't quite believe that. You are too beautiful for *any* man to resist. Only a eunuch or a man who prefers the company of other men would refuse you."

His backhanded compliment hung heavily in the silence of room, and then he asked, "Did he try?"

She swallowed hard, "Yes."

"And?"

"And what?" She bristled, embarrassment making her squirm. "Do you want all the gory details?"

"Yes." The word was flat, emotionless.

Justina closed her eyes in mortification. Then summoning an inner strength, she opened her eyes, lifted her chin and looked him squarely in the face. "All right then. I'll tell you everything. He made me come to his bedchamber every night. I was forced to strip naked and lie on his bed. He would come over and stand next to me and remove his own clothes. And then—" She stopped speaking, unable to continue, closing her eyes once more as a wave of humiliation washed over her.

"And?" This time, the one word was a tortured whisper.

Justina's eyes popped open, and she took comfort in that, as she met his piercing gaze. His eyes were bright, with some emotion she couldn't determine, but it lifted her heart and gave her the strength to carry on, "He would stand there naked, and then try to—" she made a gesture with her hand which he would understand, "But nothing. Every night for weeks I was summoned to his room. The same thing over and over. And then one night he never asked for me," she took a deep breath, "And I thank the gods every day for that small mercy…"

His mouth tightened. "He never touched you? Kissed you?"

Justina bit her lip. When she spoke her voice was husky. "No. Never."

A deafening silence filled the room until Marsallas laughed hollowly, "He was impotent. The bastard was impotent."

Justina nodded, "Yes. Yes he must have been."

"But he had so many mistresses…"

Marsallas shook his head as his voice trailed off, and Justina saw confusion flicker across his face, and her heart twisted in pity. It seemed to her as if their pasts, and their futures, were all becoming blurred, like the shadows of the night.

"So tell me, why did you lie to me when you said you wanted to be with my uncle, rather than with me all those years ago?" he eventually asked, interrupting her wayward thoughts, as he changed his line of questioning.

"I had my reasons," she said slowly.

"What reasons?" he demanded, his tone demanding an answer from her.

Justina swallowed past the lump of emotion that had lodged deep in her throat. Even after all these years the words were difficult to say. "My father had debts, huge gambling debts. He borrowed money from Quintus, and when Quintus demanded his money back he couldn't pay." She took a deep breath before she continued, lifting a hand in supplication as she went on, "So between them, they decided that *I* would be the given to him in exchange. All debts cancelled, provided I lived with him for ten years."

"But why did you lie to me?" he asked again, "You could have told me the truth when I came to your father's bakery the night I ran away."

She nodded slowly, "I know. But Quintus said that if I told

anyone about what was planned, he would have my father killed, or as he put it, '*arrange for him to have an accident*'." She drew in a tortured breath, "I couldn't let him kill my father, Marsallas. I just couldn't."

Once she'd stopped speaking, she felt a surge of emotion well up inside her, as if at last a huge weight had been lifted off her shoulders. Tears filled her eyes as she tilted her face up to his and smiled sadly, "Finally, after all these years you now know the truth."

She had given him her all. Her body. Her soul. Her love. For the one night he had demanded.

She could see by the closed expression on Marsallas's face that he was having a difficult time taking it all in. Realising that there was nothing for her to say she rose from the bed, but in her haste to leave she managed to tangle the silk sheet around her legs and hips, leaving her top half bare. Embarrassed, she turned away from him, presenting her bare back to him as she bent down to untangle herself.

Marsallas's gasp of outrage behind her was so loud that she stilled instantly.

"The scars on your back? By the gods, how did you come by them?"

His voice was hoarse with emotion, and slowly she turned and faced him. His body was tense, his eyes dark with suppressed emotion.

"Quintus," she said simply.

"He whipped you? Why in the name of Jupiter would he do that?"

For a moment Justina hesitated, but they had gone too far, and after last night she had no defences left. No more lies. "I was beaten because I ran away."

"Why? Where – *who* – were you running to Justina?"

And even though he asked the questions, Justina knew deep down that he had already worked out the answers for himself.

"I was running away to find you."

* * *

"Lampon's fetlock is sprained, I have put some salve on it but he must rest for a few days."

The words were said with a hint of sarcasm in them; sarcasm which Marsallas didn't miss. Looking at Fabius Rufus he said nothing, merely nodded, unable to stop the slight tinge of colour that stained his high cheekbones.

Fabius had every right to be angry with him. Since his return to the Circus just over a week ago he had pushed himself, and his horses, to the limit once more.

And now, as he watched Fabius strap up the horse's leg, he had every reason to be contrite. He had no excuse, of course, only his hard-headedness, his cowardliness, even.

He'd been so confused by the myriad emotions that Justina had stirred within him when she'd told him that she had tried to escape from Quintus – that he had fled back to Rome the next morning, like a dog with his tail between his legs. It had been a hard blow to the stomach to finally acknowledge that *everything* he had accused her of had been nothing but a lie. A lie fabricated by Quintus, and which she'd had no choice but to go along with in order to protect her weak father.

And if that wasn't enough, there was also another major problem. His elaborate plan for revenge had now gone – nothing but a tattered memory. Instead of the one night he'd demanded, he now found himself wanting more. One night would never be enough, he wanted her back in his bed, writhing under him, shouting out her pleasure as he took her to the heights of passion as they made love—

Love... Now why in the name of Hades had he thought of making *love* with her? It wasn't love. Because he didn't make *"love"* with women, he just had *"sex"* with them.

But you did love her once, and now she's back in your life, whether you like it or not, his mind taunted him. Yes, but her rejection of him all those years ago had cut deep, as if she had somehow wrenched open his chest, reached in and squeezed out every last drop of emotion he had left in his heart, and all that had remained to this day was an empty husk of a man.

Perhaps he should let her go. Forget about her, take another lover, even; after all, he'd had the one night he'd demanded from her.

But he dismissed those thoughts immediately, because even though he professed to be that empty husk of a man; that man *still* wanted her, *still* ached for her, and *had* to have her in his bed until he had purged himself of her once and for all.

And in order for *that* to happen she would have to become his mistress…

"Is there anything else you need, Marsallas?" The dryly spoken question jolted Marsallas out of his reverie, and he shook his head slightly, looking over to where Fabius stood watching him from the stable entrance.

"No, Fabius. Thank you." Fabius turned to leave, and Marsallas realised that he had to apologise to the younger man, "Fabius wait." Seeing the frown of annoyance on his face, which he couldn't blame him for, he walked over to the younger man and laid a hand on his shoulder in apology. "I'm sorry. You are right. I have been a fool recently. If it is any consolation I have had a lot on my mind."

"It is not for me to criticise—"

"Yes it is. I have been pushing myself, you, my horses and all those around me too much recently, and for that I apologise."

Marsallas saw Fabius relax slightly, as if he were pleased to hear that he had finally admitted the truth to himself.

"I plan to take a break for a week or so to allow my horses to recover. I would like you to take my place in the Circus in my absence."

Fabius looked shocked at Marsallas's words, as they both knew that it was considered to be a high honour to be selected as chief charioteer. "Yes, you, Fabius," he said when he saw the questioning look on his face. "Of all the men here, it is you I trust the most."

"I...I don't know what to say?" Fabius stuttered, his face pale with shock.

"You don't have to say anything, Fabius. Just don't take on too many races, eh?"

"What, like you?" Fabius said laughing, the tension between the two men disappearing.

"Especially like me!" Marsallas said dryly.

* * *

At last she had finished the last of the wax casts. Leaning back in her chair, she stretched her back out, wincing in pain as she realised she had been working for hours without a break, bent over the wax as she finished off the last of the horses' heads.

There was, she admitted, a desperation in her to finish the sculpture and leave the villa for good. But practically she knew that would be months. Casting a bronze of this size was a long process, but she was determined not to waste any time.

For seven full days now she hadn't seen Marsallas. It was as if he had vanished from the face of the earth. Vanished from her life. She didn't even know if he still remained here at the villa or had returned to Rome. *And* she had been too proud to ask any of his slaves, or even Olivia and Diogenes.

She pulled a grim face. It was as if she had served her purpose, her bargain honoured and fulfilled. She had given Marsallas what he wanted – her body for the one night he'd demanded. And although she should have realised that – prepared herself for it even – it was still a bitter potion to swallow.

Then, as if her dark thoughts had conjured him up, Justina suddenly became aware of his presence in the room. She looked up to see him watching her from the open doorway of her workroom. His blue eyes were impossibly intent as they studied her, and every emotion she had been struggling to forget came crashing back.

167

Still having the power to inflame her senses, she couldn't control the rapid beat of her heart as she looked at him. But after a few moments her resolve hardened and she stood up, chisel in her hand, lifting her head in a gesture of defiance designed to show him that she was strong, and that she *hadn't* fallen to pieces as soon as he'd left her.

"I've finished all the wax casts. I can now start on the clay moulds and then—"

"How do you fare?" he asked, interrupting her, as he moved away from the door and walked down the stairs towards her.

His question could only refer to one thing, and Justina felt the colour burn in her face, "I am well. Why shouldn't I be?"

Marsallas shrugged, walking up to her, standing so close that Justina was instantly aware of his scent, the enticing smell of him that set her pulses alight.

"No reason. Only that I took your virginity, and we had sex three times that night."

"I honoured our bargain," she said stiffly, unsure what he meant, wondering what he was thinking, planning. Was he toying with her again? Silently she mourned the wonderful lover of a week ago. The caring, gentle—.

"Yes, I know you did," he said softly, breaking into her thoughts, "But has it occurred to you that you may be pregnant? I didn't withdraw from you. My seed was inside you."

Heat seared her skin. Pregnant! The thought hadn't even occurred to her, not in the slightest, and rapidly she calculated when she'd last had her monthly flow. She very much doubted it but—

"I want you to stay here as my mistress."

Marsallas's words stopped Justina's rapid thoughts dead, and she stare open-mouthed at him. "Why?" she blurted out, instantly regretting her stupid question.

He smiled slightly, "I would have thought that was obvious enough, Justina. We are good in bed together, so why not?" He hesitated for a moment, then said softly, "I want you Justina. Like no other woman I've ever wanted, and I find that a hard thing to admit to anyone."

Justina was incapable of speech as Marsallas continued, "I told you the truth at Senator Apronius's gathering. I don't have a mistress at present. And you suit my needs."

Justina felt herself go red, not in embarrassment this time, but in anger, and finally she found her voice as she spluttered, "'I suit your needs'. Well thank *you* very much. That, coupled with the fact that I might be pregnant, you make me sound like some sort of brood mare!"

* * *

Marsallas's jaw snapped shut, a nerve working furiously. Hades! Everything he'd planned to say to her had just come out wrong! Frustration ate at him, "That isn't what I meant, Justina, and you know it," the words came out harshly, "I'm asking you to stay on here as my mistress."

For a few tense moments they just stared at each other like two adversaries spoiling for a fight until he saw Justina's shoulders slump slightly, her anger dissipating.

"For how long?" the words were spoken quietly, her tone dignified, and Marsallas felt like a prize idiot.

Raking his hand through his hair he sighed, "I don't know, Justina. Let us just take it a day at a time, shall we. See how it goes? I can't give you anything more. I want no emotional entanglements. It's the code I live by, Justina. Remember that. Always."

Justina looked away, "No I can't, Marsallas," she whispered, hurt evident in her voice. Marsallas stiffened. "Can't, or won't, Justina? There are worse things than being my mistress you know," he bit out, angrier with himself than with her. He stepped forward and lifted her chin with hard calloused fingers. "Think about it before you dismiss me out of hand. Like I said, we are good together;

it would be a pity to throw it all away for the sake of misplaced pride." And then he leaned forward and kissed her, his lips firm and determined as they pressed down on hers, demanding access to her mouth. He felt her resistance, then a heartbeat later a sense of triumph, when her mouth opened for him, letting his tongue slide in, mating with hers, a delicious parody of the intimate act they'd recently shared.

He felt a warm glow of satisfaction course through him when her arms crept up around his neck, her body pliant, as if it had overruled the logic of her mind. His hands skimmed up over her shoulders, pulling her slowly into his body. Her hair tumbled down her slim back, and he wrapped his hand in it, exerting pressure so she had no choice but to tilt her head back, exposing her neck to his mouth. His teeth nipped the sensitive skin and he felt her shiver, knowing full well that he had left his mark on her.

He felt all her muscles melt like ice in a hot sun. Suddenly pliant she moulded to the hardness of his body, and he heard her groan as the softness of her breasts pressed into the hardness of his chest.

His mouth moved downwards, until it suckled an erect nipple through the silk of her gown. This time it was he who groaned.

"Yes," he whispered, "Yes."

Then taking full advantage of the situation he pulled away, putting distance between them, watching as her eyelids fluttered open in surprise, then cloud with regret, at how brief their kiss had been.

"I told you we were good together, Justina," he whispered, "Now think about what I've said," he placed a finger on her lips when she went to open her mouth. He gave her a seductive smile that lit up his eyes. "Not now. Soon."

He watched, as a myriad expressions flitted across her face as she fought her own internal battles. Finally he said, "Desire is a strong emotion, Justina. And it's the only emotion I'm prepared to give. Remember that."

CHAPTER SEVENTEEN

"Master a visitor has arrived." Verus announced.

Marsallas frowned, raising his head from the paperwork he was working on. "Who is it?"

Verus shrugged his shoulders, "I do not know, Master. He has come to see Mistress Justina."

Marsallas frown deepened when he heard Verus say "he", and a sudden surge of jealousy coursed through him, his stomach clenching tightly with the unwelcome sensation.

Suddenly angry with himself for feeling such an emotion, he nodded at Verus and turned back to his paperwork, effectively dismissing him. But when he heard the door close behind him he stopped what he was doing and frowned in annoyance.

Who in the name of Jupiter had come to see Justina?

Standing abruptly, he walked over to the door and opened it. "What did he look like?" He shouted down the corridor at Verus's retreating back.

Verus turned at his Master's voice, "I do not know, sir. I was only passed the message that someone had arrived at the villa. I...I think he went straight to the—"

The slave never had the chance to finish his sentence because Marsallas was already heading for the stables, his stride long and purposeful.

The man was quite a few years older than either Justina or himself, but even from where he stood unseen in the darkness of the stables, he could make out that he was very handsome.

He was about the same height as him, and even though he must have been at least twenty years older than him, the stranger was still muscular, still a powerful-looking man, and once again the unwelcome sensation of jealousy surged through him.

His eyes narrowed as he watched the older man talking to Justina in what appeared to be a familiar manner. But whatever the man was telling her, Marsallas could see that it didn't appear to be good news, as Justina looked deathly pale. His jaw clenched when he saw Justina sway slightly, the stranger taking her arm to steady her.

Having seen enough, he strode towards them. "Is there anything wrong, Justina? Who is this man?" he asked, his tone abrupt, as he took the measure of the other man, a hint of challenge in his voice.

"My name is Marcus, my wife Lydia is a friend of Justina. I have come with grave news," the older man said in response to Marsallas's questions, when it became obvious that Justina was incapable of answering him.

At the man's words Marsallas relaxed slightly once he realised that Marcus was no longer a threat to him. "What has happened?" he asked Marcus, as Justina seemed to be in a total state of shock, her body trembling. Marsallas walked over to her and took her in his arms, his hands rubbing her back in a gesture of comfort.

"Mount Vesuvius has erupted. All of Herculaneum and Pompeii have been totally destroyed."

"Destroyed, but how?" Marsallas asked, shock rendering him immobile. No wonder Justina looked so ill!

"Boiling mud, many feet thick has erupted out of the mountain, entombing the entire area. There is nothing left. Everything has been destroyed. Many people are missing – presumed dead.

Hundreds injured."

"Lydia, and the rest of your family, they...they are safe?" Justina whispered, finally able to speak as she pulled out of Marsallas's embrace.

Marcus smiled gently at the young woman, "Aye. They are safe. It was Lydia who asked me to come here to tell you."

Justina lifted a trembling hand to her forehead, "Oh. Of course. I...I am being stupid."

"You are not stupid, Justina," Marsallas said quickly, his voice soothing, "It is the shock of what you have just heard that is confusing you."

Justina looked up at Marsallas, and gave him a wan smile of thanks for understanding.

"We are all safe," Marcus reiterated. "When the volcano erupted we were at our friend Anna Faustina's villa, she lives near Cumae. It escaped the wrath of the eruption, thank God."

Once Marcus had finished speaking, a long silence fell as they all contemplated the enormity of what had happened. Eventually Marsallas said, "Come, Marcus, I have been remiss, please take some refreshment. You must be exhausted after your journey."

A few minutes later they all sat drinking some honey water in the coolness of the *peristylium*. "You are more than welcome to stay here for as long as you like. My home is open to you and your family."

Marsallas saw the quick glance that Justina shot at him, and he turned slightly to capture her gaze. He felt a warm glow spread through him when she smiled at him, her eyes communicating her thanks to him.

Marcus nodded, "That is very kind of you, Marsallas. But some refreshment, that is all I ask. I must to get back to my family. They need me. Anna Faustina wants us to stay at her villa, and to be honest I think it would be best if we did for a while, until I can sort out what to do for my family."

After an hour, Marcus stood up and thanked Marsallas for his hospitality but said he had to leave now, and it was a subdued Justina and Marsallas, who watched as Marcus mounted his horse a few minutes later. Marcus looked down at Justina, who stood next to him and smiled slightly, "Remember our home is your home – wherever that may be." And with that, he lifted a hand in farewell to them both and rode out of the compound.

"Will you go?"

Justina sighed, her eyes staring sightlessly to where Marcus and his horse were now just a faint shadow in the distance. Shrugging slightly, she said, more to herself than to him, "I don't know. I really don't know."

* * *

Later that night, when the villa was finally quiet, Justina sat on the windowsill, her knees bent up to her chest in her nightly ritual. She shivered slightly, still hardly believing all that Marcus had told them.

For weeks before the eruption the whole of the area around Vesuvius had been suffering from earth tremors and many people, including Lydia, Marcus and their family had left, frightened that something terrible was going to happen. But amazingly, many people had remained, whether just plain foolhardy, or because they could not afford to leave, and unfortunately they had perished when the ash and molten mud had covered the town within the space of twenty-four hours.

According to Marcus, by the second day nothing remained of Herculaneum, the whole of the town buried in twenty feet of boiling mud. And those lucky refugees who had managed to escape had jammed the road to Neapolis, describing the horror of it all-too-shocked dignitaries that had rushed from Rome when news of the eruption had reached them.

Justina laid her head on her folded arms, tears falling unheeded down her cheeks as the emotions she had tried to suppress finally burst out. She realised she was crying for the dead, the injured, the dispossessed and the sheer enormity of what had happened. *And* if she were brutally honest with herself, she was crying for herself – worried about her future. What was she going to do now? Now, that all her plans to open a business and forge out a new life for herself lay buried in the mud of Herculaneum?

* * *

Marsallas turned over in his bed, his ears picking up a slight noise from outside his window. Rising, he went over to the window, and heard the soft sound of someone weeping.

Justina! Grim-faced he turned on his heel, strode over to his bed and picked up his discarded tunic. As soon as he opened the door to her *cubicula* he saw her instantly, silhouetted against the night sky sitting on the window ledge, her head resting on her knees, totally oblivious to anyone or anything as heart-rending sobs racked her body.

Without conscious thought he walked over to her, and wrapped his arms around her, needing, wanting, to offer her comfort. He felt her shiver at his touch, but she didn't try to pull away, merely carried on weeping.

"Shh, Justina please. You will make yourself ill," he whispered against her temple, his voice soothing, as he held her in his arms, pulling her close until he felt her tremors subside.

"I'm sorry."

"Justina, there is no need to apologise, what has happened is enough to make the strongest of men weep."

"I need to see it for myself, Marsallas," she said looking up at him, her eyes bright with the tears she had shed, imploring him to understand. "I *need* to know."

He nodded, his face grim as he stared down at her. "Yes, I can understand that."

"I want to leave tomorrow. I…I'll take Diogenes with me. If

you could let me take two horses I would be grateful—"

"No!" He said forcibly, feeling her stiffen in his arms at the loudness of his voice. Deliberately he lowered his voice, "No. I'll take you. We'll leave tomorrow, as soon as I've organised everything we'll need for the journey."

"Thank you. You are very kind."

Marsallas laugh was hollow. "You always call me kind, Justina. I'm not kind," he brushed a lock of her hair away from the curve of her cheek, his touch gentle, "You should know that by now."

He heard her laugh slightly, a small hiccup of sound, before he said, "You need to rest now, get some sleep. We have a long day ahead of us."

"No!" This time it was Justina's voice that was loud in the still-ness of the bedchamber. Then he felt her arms curl up around his neck. "Please, Marsallas. Don't leave me, I…I need—"

At her words he felt a sharp twist of longing shoot through him at what she was asking. With a swiftness of movement, he bent and lifted her into his arms striding across the room, managing to open the door with his foot before he walked down the corridor back to his bedchamber, all the while conscious of Justina nestled against his chest.

"Are you sure, Justina? Is this what you want?" he whispered as he lowered her onto his bed.

Justina looked up at him, her eyes deep pools of longing. "Yes, Marsallas. Yes. Make the pain go away. Please."

Her answer was all he needed. Placing his hands on either side of her head he lowered himself until their mouths were just touching. Her lips parted silently in open invitation and it was all he needed to fuse his mouth with hers.

Soft. Sweet. Right.

He felt her hand cup his chin, moving up to the hair at the nape of his neck. He could feel her fingers trembling. "I want you so much," he whispered against her lips, before deepening the kiss.

She arched closer, her breasts flattening against the hardness of his chest and Marsallas responded. He tangled a fist into her hair, tilting her head back, giving him better access to her mouth. Desire spread through them both, the kiss seeming to last an eternity.

Eventually he broke free, both of them panting, Justina's breasts rising and falling with the depth of her emotions. Marsallas removed their clothes, never once breaking eye contact, glorying in her response to him, her groan of pleasure, when his warm naked flesh met the softness of hers.

Justina communicated her need, her nails raking down the sleek muscles of his back, cupping his taut buttocks. He needed no further invitation, and his thigh nudged her legs apart before he slid the fullness of his erection into the tight moistness of her body.

For several minutes he moved inside her, the friction, the rhythm, causing her to gasp with pleasure time and time again. He tried to hold back, tried to make it last, but when he felt her body spasm around his, her back arching in ecstasy, Marsallas lost all conscious thought and he felt himself explode, his seed pumping deep inside her pulsing body, sending them both soaring into the night sky like eagles riding on the wind.

* * *

The dawn light filtered through the window and Justina stretched languidly. The slight movement brought her into contact with warm hard flesh that was pressed along the whole length of her back. She smiled, as she opened her eyes, twisting her head to meet his twinkling blue gaze.

Marsallas, she saw, was lying on his side, his arm propping up his head, watching her intently. Hot colour stained her cheeks as she recalled her wantonness of last night. She had practically *begged* him to make love to her, and instinctively she lifted the silk sheet higher to cover her nakedness.

At her gesture of modesty Marsallas smiled at her, before he leaned forward and kissed the back of her neck, slowly pulling the silk covers away, baring her body to his gaze: the long line of her back, the flared curves of her hips and the round softness of her buttocks.

Then he shifted, moving forwards, deliberately, bringing the fullness of his erection into the small of her back, as his lips moved to nibble the small fleshy part of her ear. "Don't hide yourself from me, Justina," he whispered, "I know every inch of your delectable body, just as you know mine."

Then he took her hand and pulled it down his body until it came into contact with his full erection. "See what you do to me? I want you again now," Marsallas said his voice gruff. Placing his hand on the fullness of her hip he turned her, so she rolled over to face him. The movement caused the necklace she was wearing to drop forward, and she saw Marsallas frown when he saw it. Lifting a hand he took the pendant in the palm of his hand, turning it so that it caught the morning light.

"My mother's ring – you still have it?" he said, his voice hoarse with suppressed emption.

Justina swallowed hard, "Yes. I've worn it every day since you gave it to me on my sixteenth birthday."

She saw Marsallas's eyes close, as a spasm of pain crossed his face. She laid a hand on his chest, feeling the rapid beat of his heart through the corded muscles, before moving lower, her hand coming to rest on the warmth of his stomach. Emboldened, she rubbed the fine hairs backwards and forwards in a gentle movement before his hand snaked out and grabbed her wrist.

"Are you sure, Justina? There's no going back."

"Yes, Marsallas," she said looking deeply into the piercing blue of his eyes.

"Then show me, Justina. Show me how much you want me."

CHAPTER EIGHTEEN

To say it was a difficult journey was an understatement.

The roads were thronged with a seething tide of humanity, as thousands of people, the homeless, the bereaved, rich, poor, merchant and slave all fled the destruction caused by Vesuvius. As well as Herculaneum and Pompeii, Oplontis and Stabiae had been totally destroyed, lost forever under a sea of molten lava, rocks, ash and boiling mud.

Justina had never felt so helpless in all her life, as they rode past all the people, desperate to get to Anna Faustina's villa. Justina had been tempted to stop so many times and help in any way she could, but she knew deep down that it would be impractical to do so. She had been relieved to see that help had already arrived, as some of the homeless had been provided with tents, and had set up make-shift camps along the roads, far enough away from Vesuvius and any further eruptions that might occur.

But as they had made their way towards Cumae, and towards Anna Faustina's villa, their journey had become much slower, hampered by the throng of people begging for help. She'd had to harden her heart towards the majority of them, as they begged for food or water as they risked having nothing left for themselves.

She had seen Marsallas give some money to several people, obviously those who had been unable to bring any of their possessions with them, and they had been able to tell them where camps had been set up that were distributing food and other essentials. Marsallas's kindness and help had been enough in some instances, as she had seen the hope come back to some of the faces.

But as much as she'd had to harden her heart, there was one instance when she just acted on instinct. They had come to a crossroads, about a day's ride from Anna Faustina's villa, and were taking a small break to tend to their horses. The heat of the midday sun was relentless, sparing neither man nor beast, and it was only when she was just about to mount her horse to journey onwards once more, that she saw her…

A small child sitting under the shade of a tree crying, the noise so heartbreaking that Justina had been moved to tears. Squinting against the fierce sunshine she saw that the child – a girl – who could not have been more than four years old was clinging to the gown of a woman who lay under the shade of a tree. The child's face and hair were covered with dirt – probably the ash from the volcano – Justina thought. Where her tears had fallen, the dirt had streaked all down her face, and large brown eyes, filled with fright and shock looked down at the woman – her mother – as she desperately tried to shake her into consciousness.

The pitiful sight was nearly Justina's undoing, and without thinking of the consequences, she dropped her horse's reins and ran over to them, unable to stop the gasp of relief that whooshed out of her chest when she saw that the woman was alive, and not dead, as she had first thought. But it was obvious that the poor woman was in some sort of deep shock as she was just lying there, oblivious to the chaos all around her, and oblivious to the needs of the child, her eyes wide open but emotionless, as she stared sightlessly up at the sky.

Kneeling down, Justina took hold of the little girl's hand, and making sure her voice was quiet, so as not to frighten her, she asked, "Is this your mama?"

The little girl stopped crying at Justina's touch, and turned towards her, her huge brown eyes full of tears as she nodded silently, her mouth trembling, trying her utmost to be big and brave.

"Good girl," she said softly, patting her lap in an unspoken gesture for the child to sit with her. The little girl needed no second invitation and took the warmth and comfort that Justina offered, moving into her arms without a moment's hesitation, desperate for human companionship, for some act of kindness.

Justina let her settle for a few minutes, before she leaned forward and took the woman's hand, amazed that it could feel so cold in the blazing heat of the afternoon sunshine. Unsure what to do for the best, Justina started to stroke the cold skin, her movements gentle, hoping that the rhythmic action might stimulate the prone woman in some way.

For several minutes Justina continued with her task, until she was rewarded for her efforts when she felt the woman move slightly. Glancing at her face she breathed a sigh of relief when she saw that the woman was looking at her, her eyes, thankfully, having lost their haunted look.

Smiling down at her she said quietly, "My name is Justina. Is there anything I can do to help? Your daughter is very worried about you." The woman appeared to be only a few years older than herself. For a moment Justina thought that she wasn't going to answer her, but then, her voice hesitant and hoarse with the ash and dust she must have swallowed, she whispered, "Do you know where my husband is?"

Justina had to fight back her tears at the woman's words, and shook her head.

"I...I begged him not to go, but he wouldn't listen to me. He...he said he had to help," the woman said, the faraway look back in her eyes as she remembered. But then her face twisted in pain, "But he should have stayed with *us*, not left, not gone back into that...that inferno. Oh, I know I'm being selfish," she cried, looking up at Justina, tears rolling down her face, "But I want my husband back. *I* need him. *Claudia* needs him." She looked at her daughter, sitting quietly on Justina's lap, before lifting her hand out towards her, and the little girl needing no further invitation flew out of Justina's lap and into her mother's arms. For a few minutes Justina watched as mother and daughter hugged each other, the woman rocking backwards and forwards as tears of sorrow fell unheeded down her face.

Eventually the woman composed herself, and with a slight flush on her cheeks looked over to where Justina still knelt on the dry grass, "You have been most kind, and I'm sorry for burdening you—"

"You have no need to be sorry for anything, truly." Justina said quietly, cutting off her words. "Is there anything I can do to help you and your daughter?"

"I...I would beg a little food for her, she is hungry and frightened," the woman said hesitantly.

"Of course. I will go and fetch you some," Justina said, getting up quickly before turning and nearly knocking over Marsallas, who she saw, with some embarrassment, was standing right next to her.

Marsallas! She had completely forgotten about him, and she flushed in mortification for ignoring him. Thankfully, if he had anything to say on the matter he kept quiet, his face sombre as he took in the situation.

"Could we spare a little food and water?" she asked. At his slight nod, she felt the pressure lift from her shoulders. She watched as he walked over to his horse and took out some of their provisions from his saddlebag, before returning with a small loaf of bread and some cheese.

The woman, who Justina found out later was called Phoebe, was so grateful that she burst into tears again, and Justina spent a further ten minutes comforting her before she could persuade her, and Claudia, to eat some food. Once they had finished eating there was nothing more Justina and Marsallas could do for them, and feeling somewhat helpless Justina stood up from where she had been sitting by the grass verge.

She so wanted to help them further, having been deeply moved by the sadness in the little girl's eyes when it was apparent that they would have to leave, but not having any money on her, she had felt helpless. Turning to Marsallas she asked quietly, "I would not normally ask, but could you spare her some money? She has nothing."

Justina felt a surge of love flow through her when Marsallas nodded and went over to where the woman and child lay. She saw him kneel down and speak to Phoebe before he passed her a small pouch with some money in it. For a few minutes he spoke quietly to the woman, and Justina couldn't help but wonder what he was saying to her, as the woman was looking up at him with a look of hope, and surprise, on her face.

It was only later, as they rode away from them, that she found out. Marsallas had offered Phoebe and her daughter a home for as long as she wished at his villa and with the money he had given her she should be able to obtain transport and a safe passage to get there.

"Oh thank you, Marsallas. You are so kind, I don't know what to say."

Marsallas smiled at her before saying, "You don't need to say anything. Just promise me that you won't adopt *all* the people we come across. My villa isn't big enough to accommodate everybody, no matter how bad the situation is!"

For the rest of the day they carried on with their journey, a journey hampered further as the swell of the homeless became heavier and heavier as they got nearer to Vesuvius. Eventually, Marsallas called a halt for the day, for which Justina was silently thankful. The journey so far had been emotionally, as well as physically, taxing and she ached so much that she thought she might never be able to stand straight. She hadn't said anything to Marsallas about it, but in all honesty she was unused to riding a horse, and definitely not used to riding for hours on end!

It soon become obvious that there was little chance of securing any accommodation in the inns along the way as every one of them was full to capacity. So they had little choice but to sleep under the stars with their horses, after Marsallas had eventually found a suitable site to make camp for the night.

The camp was just a small space in a field just off the main road which they had to share with many other people. But thankfully, there was a small lake nearby where they could get water for the horses and themselves. Justina looked at the cool water longingly, wishing that she could take a bath and wash away all the dust that clogged her skin and clothes. But her wistful gaze left the lake. There would probably be little hope of bathing, and she concentrated on helping Marsallas set up their simple camp, working together in a companionable silence.

Later they shared some of the food between them, and once they had finished eating Justina went down to the lake to rinse off the wooden plates they had used, and to wash away the dirt from her hands and face as best she could. After she had returned from the lake it was Marsallas's turn, and she watched him from under her long lashes as he led their horses down the water's edge to drink.

She held back a sigh as she watched his strong muscular body stride away, her gaze wandering over the breadth of his shoulders down over his muscular back and slim hips to the long length of his tanned legs. As she took her fill of him she wondered if she would ever tire of watching him, and when she finally looked away she saw that other women, both young and old, were watching him as well. Justina's mouth twisted. He was a man no woman could resist, and once again a feeling of jealousy came over her as she thought of him with other women.

Suddenly, she was annoyed with herself. She realised she wasn't being rational. She had no clame over Marsallas apart from being his latest lover. No claim at all. Their relationship wasn't based on exclusivity – hadn't Claudetta warned her of that? Yes, he had made love to her – but that was as far as it went. And although he had offered her a position as his latest mistress, who knew how long it would last? She knew nothing about him really.

He was an enigma. For all she knew she could be one of many. Hadn't he mocked her all those months ago about how much he was in demand with the women of Rome?

Justina sighed, forcing her thoughts away from what might be, to the right now. There was a humanitarian crisis of such magnitude going on all around her, and all she could think of was Marsallas making love to her!

Rising from where she sat on the ground, she busied herself putting away the things they didn't need, in preparation for when they would leave in the morning. She then took her blanket and tried to make herself comfortable on the hard ground, thankful that the evening was coming to an end and darkness was falling rapidly over the area. She didn't want to think about Marsallas any more, it was too painful, too raw, and shifting her weight to a more comfortable position she willed herself to sleep.

But after about ten minutes of tossing and turning on the sun-baked ground, she realised that trying to sleep was impossible, as she was being kept awake by the noises from the surrounding camps. And if she was honest with herself, she missed Marsallas's presence next to her. She was being silly, she knew that after all he had only gone to bathe. But still, she only relaxed when she saw him walking towards her, his steps light so as not to disturb her. She heard him bed down nearby, and after about half an hour the noise from the surrounding camp seemed to die down for the night, and a quietness fell over the area

Finally, Justina fell into a fitful sleep only to be awakened a short while later by the shrill cry of a baby, which rent the still night air. She heard the mother of the child trying to sooth the fractious child, and after ten minutes or so the baby must have gone back to sleep. Unfortunately for Justina she never did, and looking over to her left, she could see Marsallas lying nearby on his pallet, his silhouette outlined by the light from the moon.

She had to resist the urge to go over to him, to lie next to him, to have him take her in his arms, his strength wrapped around her, comforting her, and for him to promise that he would never leave her, for them to have a future together.

She knew she was being stupid to wish for such a thing; but she so desperately wanted him that she knew she wasn't thinking rationally. It was obvious to her that there could be no future between them, he still harboured a deep resentment against her for betraying him all those years ago. And although he now knew the truth of what had happened, there was still too much past between them to ever make it right.

CHAPTER NINETEEN

If it was chaos on the roads, then it was equally chaotic when they finally reached Anna Faustina's villa.

As soon as they had entered the courtyard, Justina couldn't hold back her gasp of shock as they were met by a tidal wave of people. Servants rushed around with pots of water, food and medicines, tending to what appeared to Justina's eyes to be around fifty people, all of them obviously injured as they lay or sat in the courtyard, taking up every available inch of space.

As her eyes searched the faces, she saw with some relief Lydia's familiar slim form leaning over the slumped figure of a woman as she bandaged her head. Even from where she sat on her horse, she could tell that her touch was gentle and soothing. Lydia seemed to exude a calming presence over all those that she healed, and Justina smiled as she remembered how she had helped her all those years ago...

* * *

"Oh, Justina, I am so glad to see you!" Lydia said, before embracing Justina, hugging her so hard and with such intensity, that she felt tears spring to her eyes at the warmth of her welcome.

Finally, they pulled away and Justina turned to where Marsallas stood next to her. Feeling slightly nervous, she introduced him, "Lydia, this is Marsallas, Quintus's nephew. Marsallas, this is my friend, Lydia." She held her breath when Marsallas took Lydia's hand and lifted it to his mouth.

"Your husband did not exaggerate your beauty, Lydia," he murmured as he kissed the back of her hand, "I am honoured to meet you."

Lydia laughed, her green eyes twinkling at the compliment. "Marcus is incorrigible. If I weren't so old I would blush! But thank you for the compliment, and welcome, Marsallas."

Then her face sobered, "Did you have a good journey? What news can you bring?"

But before either of them could answer her question they were joined by Marcus. Justina saw the look that passed between husband and wife, saw their love for each other, and momentarily she envied how their love transcended everything.

"Lydia, I'm sure Marsallas and Justina are too tired to answer your questions. They have had a long journey."

Lydia clapped her hands, exclaiming, "Oh, I'm so remiss. Come, come, both of you. There are refreshments inside."

* * *

He leaned back against the smooth tiles of the bath, letting the heat warm his aching muscles.

Sighing, he closed his eyes and imagined Justina joining him. Would the heat of the room bring about a rosy glow to her body? He rather imagined it would. The steam would cause her hair to curl, he was sure of that too. He licked his lower lips, as he imagined her walking naked towards him, the water lapping at her thighs and hips as she came towards him. He imagined his wet hands cupping the fullness of her breasts, the water making her nipples pebble in arousal. Heat pooled in his groin and he groaned in frustration. She was driving him mad! His body was so erect, so hard it was painful.

But he was also exhausted. He couldn't have slept for more than five hours in the three days they'd taken to reach the villa. He'd lain awake, hour after hour, in the darkness, ears tuned to each and every sound, totally alert to anything that might compromise his, or more importantly, Justina's safety, as they made their journey north.

He had been shocked to the core at the scenes of desolation that had greeted them as they travelled to Anna Faustina's villa. And although the majority of the people flooding the roads were to be pitied, he knew instinctively that evil always follows destruction, and there would be people unscrupulous enough to prey on the weak. And as long as he had a breath left in his body, he had silently vowed to protect Justina.

* * *

"Marsallas! May I beg a moment of your time?"

Marsallas turned to see Justina hurrying down the corridor towards him, the light from the oil lamps that lit the darkness illuminating her silhouette. As she approached, he drank in her beauty, the slightly flushed face, the full rosy lips, slightly parted, the flush of youth on her skin, and the grey of her eyes darkened with emotion. To say she looked beautiful was an understatement, and his eyes fell from her face, taking in the silk *stola* of dark blue she wore, the fabric falling from the fullness of her breasts. It was as if the silk caressed her, and he had to fight the urge to pull her into his arms, to kiss her. His stomach clenched with reaction, with longing for her, with the need to bury himself deep inside—

"Marsallas!" She repeated, "May I have a word in private?"

Jolted out of his wicked thoughts, he looked over his shoulder, seeing the *peristylium* nearby. He placed his hand on the small of her back, and guided her out into the darkness of the colonnaded garden, aware of her slight shiver when he touched her. Was the heat of his hand, burning through the gossamer silk of her *stola*, making her yearn for the feel of his hands on her bare flesh? *He hoped so*. Once they were seated on a bench under one of the trees, Marsallas asked, "Now tell me, what is wrong?"

Justina shook her head slightly, "There is nothing wrong, really. I just wanted to speak to you about Lydia and Marcus...and the rest of their family." He was slightly taken aback by the nervous tone in her voice and raised an eyebrow for her to continue.

"Well...well there is no easy way to say what I am going to say so I'll just say it as it is." Justina said, her words tumbling out, "Lydia and Marcus...and the rest of the family...well they are Christians... and I just wanted to... to let you know...so you know..."

She stopped speaking, her words trailing off disjointedly.

Marsallas said nothing for a moment, his mind recalling all he knew of the new secret religious sect. Then he took her hands – trembling hands he noticed – and said quietly, "I'm not a bigot, Justina. It does not matter what faith your friends are. They have shown me – *us* – nothing but kindness ever since we arrived here, so as far as I am concerned they are my friends also." Seeing the relief on her face, he continued, "I'm assuming Anna Faustina is one of these Christians too?"

Justina nodded, "As are all in the villa. There are no slaves here. They have all been given their freedom."

Marsallas nodded slowly, "I wouldn't do anything to compromise your friend's faith, and ultimately their safety. You can trust me."

Justina's shoulders slumped in relief, the tension leaving her. "Thank you, Marsallas. It means a lot to me and...and I do trust you."

Her words were heartfelt, and he couldn't stop himself when he leaned forward and gently kissed her. Her lips tasted so sweet. It seemed an age since he'd last kissed her, and unable to stop, he took hold of her upper arms and pulled her forward, deepening the kiss.

course," she said with a small twist of her lips, "But Marcus over-ruled me, saying it would be futile to take on too much, insisting that it was better to give quality care to some, rather than poor care to many." Lydia smiled sadly, before continuing, "He is right, of course. But it doesn't make it any easier to bear."

"And your supplies? How are they holding out?"

"Now that is something I *am* worried about," Lydia sighed deeply, "My supplies of opium are rapidly diminishing, with so many burn patients I am having to use a lot of it for the pain."

"I could go to Rome and get some."

Both women turned to see Marsallas standing in the shadows, a frown of concern on his face, "I could go tomorrow morning, and I would be back in a few days. I know Senator Lucius Apronius, and I'm sure that if I explained what you were doing here, there would be no problem in securing more opium."

"Marsallas that is very kind of you. I knew Senator Lucius Apronius and he always came across as a kindly man," Anna Faustina said, overhearing the conversation, and seeking to reassure Lydia.

"I...I...don't know," Lydia hesitated, still unsure.

"I would not compromise your position here, Lydia," Marsallas said quietly. "You know we are Christians?" Lydia asked, her voice incredulous, immediately understanding what Marsallas was saying. At his slight nod, her shoulders slumped in relief.

"It is very kind of you to offer, Marsallas," Lydia finally said, "It would help enormously to have extra opium."

Marsallas smiled, "Good. I'll leave in the morning." He then turned to Justina, "By the way, once I get back from Rome I intend to hire a boat. I promised you that I would take you to see Herculaneum. Doing it by sea is by far the safest way."

* * *

Marsallas returned to the villa from Rome four days later, having

193

ridden hard and fast to get back. The hour was late and he was exhausted, but at the same time strangely buoyant at the thought of being back and seeing Justina. But as he walked into the *triclinium* his mood changed. He could tell by the atmosphere there that something was amiss. Everyone looked emotionally drained and subdued.

He hesitated, standing silently at the door, until Justina looked up, suddenly aware of his presence.

"Marsallas. You're back!" She got up off her couch and rushed over to his side, a smile of welcome on her face. Her words seemed to galvanise the others and they stood up to welcome him. A few minutes later he found himself relaxing on one of the couches, eating some food and telling them all that had happened in Rome.

"...So when I told Senator Apronius what you were doing, he was adamant that we should tell the Emperor, and sure enough the next morning, both the Senator and I were granted a private audience."

"The Emperor. Really!" they all chorused at once, and Marsallas smiled slightly at their reactions.

"Yes. The Emperor has been most concerned to hear of the terrible eruption, and any news about what is happening he is taking very seriously."

"Oh, that is good to hear, Marsallas. Sometimes we are so busy tending to the injured, it feels as if no one cares." Lydia said quietly, echoing what they all thought.

Marsallas nodded in sympathy, "I understand. But when I told him of your work here at the villa he promised to send opium and other medicines to help as soon as possible. I have come back with four saddlebags of opium for you to be going on with."

"Oh Marsallas, that is wonderful news! We are in very short supply at the moment, and were getting desperate." Justina said eventually, when it was obvious that Lydia was too overwhelmed to speak.

"That is not all," Marsallas said, his voice earnest, before he turned to Anna Faustina, who was sitting across from him, "The Emperor also said that he felt humbled by what you were doing to help the injured, and he has called your villa the 'Villa of Hope.'"

* * *

Once the evening meal had finished, Justina accompanied Marsallas to the stables to help him bring in the opium, which was still in his saddlebags. Walking side by side across the courtyard, Justina couldn't help the quiver of awareness that assailed her at the closeness of his body. Although they had been incredibly busy at the villa tending to the sick, there wasn't an hour that had gone by when she hadn't thought of him.

As they entered the stables, the dimness lit only by one oil lamp, Marsallas stopped and took hold of Justina's hand. The warmth of his strong hand holding hers caused her to shiver in need. Then with his other hand he tipped her chin upwards so he could gaze into her eyes, "Did you miss me, Justina? Because I missed you, desperately," he whispered softly.

She felt herself blush, but before she could answer his face grew serious, "You look tired, have you been pushing yourself too hard?"

Justina swallowed past the lump of emotion that threatened to clog her throat before she shook her head slightly. "I'm fine Marsallas. It's…it's just that we lost a patient today, a young girl. The burns she suffered were too great for Lydia to heal. It hit us all hard."

Marsallas said nothing, but nodded his head in understanding, and Justina continued, "But your news tonight helped cheer everyone up, as well as the amount of opium you were able to bring."

"I'm glad." He came closer, his eyes dark with suppressed emotion, and her heart kicked against her chest when his head lowered towards hers and captured her mouth with his. Her bones turned molten, as liquid desire pulsed through her when he deepened the kiss, coaxing her lips apart, and it was *everything* she needed to wipe out all the pain and desolation around them.

It was only when they heard the muted shout of someone in the courtyard that he broke off the kiss, and for an age they stood there, wrapped in each other's arms until Marsallas pulled away to look down at her. He trailed one finger down the smoothness of her cheek before he murmured, "Have you thought about what you are going to do in the future?"

The words were like a splash of cold water and she stiffened, anger coursing through her. "I have been far too busy to think about being your mistress, Marsallas, there are—" she broke off, breathing heavily, "…there are far more important things going on at the moment."

Hot colour surged along his cheekbones, and she saw his jaw clamp shut, "That is not what I meant. I—"

"Didn't you, Marsallas?" Justina interjected, too angry to listen. Neither spoke for a moment, and Justina saw that his face had closed, an implacable mask, impossible to read, and she took his silence as the proof she needed. All she was to him was a body, someone to assuage his needs. A mistress for as long as he needed her.

Hurt pride made her words harsh as she lashed out, "You are so full of hate it has blinded you. You will turn out *exactly* like Quintus: bitter, resentful, never trusting, never letting go of the past. Hatred has festered inside you for so long." She hesitated for a moment, "I…I can't be with a man who is like that. I've lived for too long with a man like that." She felt tears threaten, but ruthlessly stamped them down, "But that is Roman society isn't it? Men rule. Women are nothing, merely there to satisfy your needs. But *I* want more than that. I *can* have more than that. I can sculpt, make a name for myself. Be free to do what *I* want for the first time in my life."

Exhausted, she stopped speaking. She had said enough. Finally, she had faced the truth of their relationship. He had made love to her with his body, but not with his heart.

And that, she realised, was something she wasn't prepared to put up with. She just couldn't live like that, never knowing from one day to another if it was going to be their last. Living with the uncertainty, waiting for him to tell her that he'd tired of her, just as he had done with all his previous lovers.

Was she mad to want it all? Shouldn't she just take what he offered? But he had made it quite clear hadn't he? No emotional involvement – ever.

And she wanted so very much more. Pain lanced through her as she faced the truth of what she had to do. She loved him unequivocally, *that* refused to be squashed, but she *couldn't* become his mistress and let her heart be broken a second time.

A thunderous silence fell between them, before Marsallas said, "I'm not such an insensitive bastard, Justina, that I demand that you leave here and return to my villa to fulfil my needs."

The bitterness of his words made Justina's stomach plummet. "I...I don't—"

"Is something wrong, Justina? Marsallas?"

Justina's head whipped around to see Lydia standing at the stable door, concern etched on her face.

A long silence fell between the three of them before Marsallas answered her question. "There is nothing wrong, Lydia. I was just informing Justina that I have arranged for a boat to take us to Herculaneum tomorrow. It leaves at the fifth hour." Then he bowed stiffly to both women, and strode out of the stables.

* * *

Marsallas punched his fist against his bedroom wall, the pain a welcome relief.

Hatred has festered in you for so long.

Justina's words kept going round and round in his head, and bile roiled in his stomach, making him feel sick.

Hades! She was right, of course. Hatred, revenge, call it what you like, had eaten away at him, and he had been blinded by it for so long. He should have realised that Quintus was up to no good. But anger had blinded him, and when she hadn't denied any of his accusations he had taken her silence as an admission of guilt, believing that she had wanted his wealth and position more than him. And all the while she had endured such pain at Quintus's cruel hands.

But she'd still managed to be strong, retain some inner strength somehow. Guilt lay heavily in his stomach, like rancid wine. He should have realised the truth when he had discovered that she had been a virgin.

"By the gods you are a fool!" He cursed to himself. Raking a hand through his hair in agitation, he strode over to a low table and poured some water into a goblet, noticing that his hand shook with the force of his emotions. And that, he realised with a start, was the root of the problem. He had absolutely no idea how to reveal his feelings to her, because he'd suppressed them so ruthlessly, and for so long now.

He'd lost her. She had made her position clear, and deep down he couldn't, *didn't*, blame her. She deserved better. A virtual prisoner by Quintus's hand, she deserved her freedom, to finally do what she wanted. He could see that.

But he still wanted her. Loved her.

"Yes," he hissed, when he realised the enormity of what he'd just admitted to himself. He *did* love her. He'd resisted for so long, when the truth had been there all along, staring him in the face. *It had always been her.* Ever since she had come back into his life he'd tried to persuade himself that it was just lust that he felt for her. But he'd just been fooling himself. The simple truth was... he'd never stopped loving her.

Marsallas took a long deep breath. It was time he made peace with his past. Time he went after what *really* mattered in his life. Justina. *She* was what he wanted more than anything else.

The only problem was, how in the name of Jupiter was he going to convince her otherwise? Had he left it too late..?

CHAPTER TWENTY

Justina looked at the scene of devastation laid out before her, hardly able to take it all in. It was as if some macabre play had been put on for all to see. A play of such spectacular horror that it defied belief. Surely this couldn't be real? It had to be a nightmare, a bad dream, and wanting it to end she closed her eyes to block it out.

But the slight swell of the boat, the flapping of the wind in the sails told her otherwise and her eyes snapped open. This was no dream. This was reality.

Nothing remained of Herculaneum, or of Pompeii, for that matter. Nothing to show that they had once been thriving towns, home to thousands of people. Vesuvius, the mountain she had lived next to all her life, had sucked up all the hot entrails of the underworld and thrust them upwards into the heavens, before falling back to earth and covering all the surrounding area in a heaving mass of stones, ash, lava and boiling mud.

Boiling mud that had flown down the mountainside and entombed the whole of the town before it had met the coldness of the Mediterranean Sea, where it had solidified in a seething mass of hissing steam to create an artificial peninsula some one thousand feet from what had originally been the coastline. The coastline villa, where she and Marsallas had lived; the most sumptuous villa in the whole of Herculaneum, now lost forever.

The enormity of it all caused her to sway, and she had to tighten her grip on the wooden railings of the boat to stop herself from falling.

"Are you ill, Justina?"

Marsallas! She hadn't even been aware of him standing next to her. She finally managed to speak, "No...no I'm fine." She heard the stiffness in her voice. Hardly surprising really, as this was the first time she had spoken to him since last night. Their trip from Anna Faustina's villa to the port of Misenum this morning had been conducted in total silence.

She looked at him for the first time since they had boarded the boat, and her heart stilled momentarily. He looked haggard, drawn, the skin stretched tight across his cheekbones, his lips thin lines of strain, and her heart suddenly lurched when she saw the depth of pain in his eyes.

"Nothing remains," Marsallas said eventually, his voice raw. "You could have been there. Lost to me forever."

Justina tried to speak, but she was incapable of words. Had she had heard him correctly? Her heart beat faster, hope filling her as she stared up at him, willing him to continue.

"Do you know how many people there are in my life, Justina?" He gave a short, harsh, laugh. "None. No one. And why? Because I *wanted* it that way, that's why. You were right in what you said yesterday. I *am* bitter and twisted. I wanted to punish you so badly for what had happened in the past.

I promised myself that I would take your body and discard you, as I thought you had discarded me. Ever since I left Herculaneum I've been consumed by hatred. Hatred for you. Hatred for my uncle. I was driven by it. It's made me the man I am today," he drew in a ragged breath, before lowering his voice, "That night" – his face worked "that night I made love to you. Once I realised that you were a virgin, I knew I could never let you go. And it scared me, made me angry. It wasn't supposed to be like *that*." He went on raggedly, "I was just going to take your body. Have my revenge against you."

He shut his eyes for a moment and then opened them, his gaze fierce, the intensity of it making her breath catch.

"I wanted to hate you, wanted to punish you. Oh, how I tried, believe me. But there was always something deep inside me that fought against it. And do you know what it is?"

She shook her head, incapable of speech, and he smiled the briefest of smiles, before he lifted his hand and cupped the side of her jaw, the roughness of his fingers against her skin sending shivers down her spine.

"It's love, Justina. I love you. I always have. I made myself suppress it, refused to acknowledge it. But ever since you've come back into my life – that day at the Circus – I've not been able to get you out of my head. It's as if the love had lain dormant, just like that mountain over there had for years," he said, gesturing with his head towards the smoking volcano in the distance. "I know I've treated you badly, and I can't take that back...but...but what I can do is promise you that I will always love you. All I ask is that you give me a second chance to prove it to you."

He stopped speaking, his chest rising and falling deeply as he took in a deep breath. Then he said, his voice intense, "Be my wife. My love. My all. Fill my life, Justina, because it's been empty for too long."

Justina looked up at him, tears shining in her eyes, when she saw that his eyes were almost black with emotion at what he'd just revealed to her. She knew it must have taken a lot for him to share those feelings with her, to confess his innermost fears.

So she smiled up at him and whispered, "My life would be empty too without you, Marsallas."

It was all he needed to hear and he pulled her gently towards him and lowered his head, his mouth touching hers, the kiss long and sweet. Eventually it ended and he reluctantly pulled away. Justina looked up at him, her face alight with hope, her voice husky, "I love you too, Marsallas. I always have, and I always will." Justina lifted a hand, her palm resting on the hard planes of his face, communicating her feelings to him, a radiant smile illuminating her face.

"Marry me, Justina. I want you to come back to my villa and make it a home. I can't live without you. You make me whole, make me feel alive, make me *want* to live again." There was a break in his voice, an uncertainty that made Justina's throat tighten. "Will you Justina? Will you marry me?" She heard the sudden fierceness of his words, saw his eyes flare with longing.

Sucking in a deep breath, she took one final look over her shoulder at what had been her birthplace, now lost forever under a sea of mud, before she turned back to face him and whispered, "Yes, Marsallas. I will marry you. Take me home."

Then he kissed her again, and she knew that in Marsallas she had her future. A life full of possibilities. He would let her sculpt, let her fulfil her potential. And eventually they would have children. And all the while she knew that she would have his love. An endless, boundless supply of it.

They had conquered their pasts, and they were about to celebrate their futures. Together. Forever. For always.

EPILOGUE

"It's magnificent. You are magnificent."

The words whispered in her ear caused her to shiver. Justina turned and looked up into the handsome face of her adoring husband.

"It's not bad."

"Not bad!" Shaking his head, Marsallas looked up at the bronze statue that sat above the entrance arch of the Circus Maximus.

"I should have spent more time on it. I hurried some of the castings at the end."

"You've been distracted. I accept that. But still, the statue is magnificent. All of Rome is talking about how wonderful it is. How talented *you* are." Marsallas leaned forward, his mouth trailing down to the softness of her neck.

"Umm. I have been distracted," she murmured, "A new husband has that effect on a woman." She gasped when his teeth nipped at her skin, turning her bones to molten wax. Turning, she slipped her arms around Marsallas's neck, lifting her mouth up for his kiss.

"I love you," Marsallas whispered, when the kiss finally ended, and he'd stepped away from her. His eyes went to the bronze statue once more. "Tomorrow I race my last race here. And then we begin the next chapter of our lives." His hand reached down to clasp hers, bringing them both up to rest on her rounded stomach, heavily swollen with child.

"You coming back into my life finally made me realise what I want most in life. You. As my wife, as the mother of my children, but most importantly, by my side, forever."

Lightning Source UK Ltd.
Milton Keynes UK
UKHW03f1228230318
319943UK00002B/399/P